I0769488

DON'T SHOOT *the messenger*

Hazard Falls
Book 2

SAMANTHA COLE

Author's Note

Any information regarding persons or places has been used with creative literary license so there may be discrepancies between fiction and reality. The missions and personal qualities of members of the military and law enforcement within have been created to enhance the story and, again, may be exaggerated and not coincide with reality.

The author has full respect for the members of the United States military and the varied members of law enforcement and thanks them for their continuing service to making this country as safe and free as possible.

Chapter 1

T. Carter settled back on the couch in the living room of the hotel suite he'd stayed in for the past twenty-five days and watched Grant Hadley pace back and forth. Although the CIA spook was released from the US military hospital in Landstuhl, Germany, yesterday, Hadley was a shell of his former self. Despite being rehydrated and fed healthy food, his clothes hung from his thin frame, and his sallow skin still hadn't returned to normal. That's what happens when you spend over six years in a North Korean prison camp for espionage while the United States government thinks you're dead.

Carter still tried to wrap his brain around the fact that his buddy was alive and not thousands of feet below the surface in the Sea of Japan. He'd been too far away to rescue the man he thought was Hadley after seeing a body, wrapped in a tarp with weights attached, tossed into one of the deepest trenches found in those waters. Even if he'd had SCUBA gear with him, Carter never would have reached the area in time after agents from the Ministry of State Security— MSS—had finally headed their cabin cruiser inland again. He'd been on his own, in a much smaller boat, with only two handguns and a KABAR knife, and wouldn't have stood a chance against five heavily armed and highly trained MSS agents.

Carter worked as an operative for Deimos, a US black ops agency. Currently, he waited for his CIA counterpart to ask the questions he'd been dreading. In fact, he was surprised they hadn't come up during the past three weeks of debriefing and rehabilitation Hadley had gone through.

A few times since the rescue op, Carter had almost slipped and called the other man Evan Walker, which had been his main undercover persona. It was the only reason Hadley could return to the US using his real surname.

Sitting in a chair across the coffee table from Carter, Hadley leaned forward and rested his elbows on his knees. His scraggly beard and mustache had been shaved off, and his thin, dark-brown hair had been trimmed by a barber yesterday after his release from the hospital. He looked far different from the dirty, raggedly clothed, emaciated man Carter and a team of retired Navy SEALs had rescued, but his hazel eyes still appeared sunken. He took two deep breaths, then asked coarsely, "How is she? How did she take it?"

Carter bit his bottom lip for a moment before replying. *She* was Blair Canterfield, the woman Hadley had been engaged to. The woman who thought her fiancé was a Secret Service agent temporarily assigned to the ambassador to South Korea six years ago. The woman the US government had lied to, telling her Hadley had fallen overboard from a yacht he was on with his charge during a storm, and his body hadn't been recovered. The woman who had no clue Hadley was, in fact, alive.

"She's doing okay—took it really hard, but . . ." He couldn't finish the sentence, needing the other man to ask each question at his own pace.

There was a heavy pause as Hadley stared at Carter before continuing. "Has she moved on? I mean, has she . . ."

"She moved back to Hazard Falls not long after the memorial service they had for you . . . she's married."

The man nodded as resignation appeared in his eyes. "I'm not surprised—Blair's a beautiful woman, and it's . . . it's been a long time—but I was hoping . . ." He ran a hand down his face. "Who? Someone from Hazard? Do I know him?"

Here it came. The hardest thing Carter had to tell his old friend. "Grant . . . she's married to Drake."

Hadley froze, stunned to silence, as Carter waited

for the inevitable words of disbelief followed by an explosion.

Shaking his head, Hadley said, "This is no time for jokes, jackass." He stood and paced back and forth again. "No . . . no fucking way."

"I'm not joking, man. I'm sorry."

He stopped in front of Carter and put his hands on his hips. "Blair married Drake? She married my fucking brother?" When Carter nodded, Hadley glared and asked, "When? When, damn it!"

The black-ops agent sighed. Shit, he hated to be the one doing this, but he owed it to Hadley. He could've lied, but things would have been worse if the man had discovered the truth later. Blair had probably been his lifeline over the past six years, the main reason he'd survived the hellhole he'd been in—he wouldn't let her go without knowing all the facts. Carter took a deep breath and let it out. "Six weeks after the funeral."

"The fuck you say!"

Hadley lunged at Carter with rage-filled eyes, but the Deimos spy was far quicker, leaping up and side-stepping out of the way. Hadley landed partially on the couch, his knees hitting the floor, and he struggled to stand. Once on his feet again, he swung at his target, who easily blocked the fist coming toward his face. Carter spun him around, tucked his hands under Hadley's armpits, and put him in a headlock—not for Carter's protection, but to keep the broken man from harming himself.

"Get off me! Get the fuck off me, you bastard!"

Bucking, twisting, and kicking, Hadley made every effort to break the hold, but his weakened body was no match against the other man's physically fit one. He finally gave up, and his knees buckled. Tears rolled down his face, and a sob ripped from his chest as Carter lowered him to the floor, relaxing his grip but not completely letting go. "I'm sorry, Grant. I'm so sorry."

For a few minutes, Carter silently allowed the other man to let it all out—the grief, the rage, the fear he'd never be rescued that'd plagued him for so long, and the relief when he'd realized the rescue was really happening and wasn't a dream. This was the first time Hadley had broken down since Carter and his team had found him in a North Korean mountainside prison camp. He'd been living in a dirty cage, unfit for any animal, covered in scars and cigarette burns in various stages of healing, The US operatives had killed every one of his fourteen captors and had also rescued a French national, two South Koreans, and a member of the UK's MI6. Those men, all in a similar condition to Hadley, had each been returned to their respective countries under a cloak of secrecy. There hadn't been a single mention of the dead North Korean soldiers left in the mountains on any media outlet, which meant it'd been covered up.

Carter had been shocked when his boss called him with the news that a man who looked eerily like

Hadley had been spotted and photographed by an MSS mole who'd passed the information onto his Deimos handler. Upon seeing the images, guilt and remorse had overwhelmed Carter. He hadn't taken things at face value all those years ago. Still, the investigation that'd followed, after seeing the body tossed overboard, hadn't turned up anything to dispute the belief that Hadley had ended up at the bottom of the sea.

Seven or eight minutes passed before Hadley caught his breath and stopped sobbing. Carter let him go and got to his feet as the other man slowly stood and wiped his face with his bare hands. "Tell me . . . tell me the rest. There's more, isn't there?"

Hadley's mind was surprisingly sharp after all he'd been through. Carter nodded. "There is."

Instead of launching into the next bit of intel, he had to report, he strode over to the suite's wet bar and poured the expensive Macallan Fine Oak scotch he preferred into two lowball glasses. He handed one to Hadley, who'd slumped into the chair again, then returned to his seat on the couch. Taking a sip, he relished the familiar burn and waited for the other man to stop coughing after knocking back a swig of the amber liquid.

Hadley looked at him. His voice was even raspier than before. "Tell me."

"The reason Blair and Drake got married—she was three and a half months pregnant."

The man's brow furrowed in confusion, but not for

long as the true meaning of Carter's words sunk into his brain. "Pregnant? I . . . she was pregnant . . . with my child?"

He nodded. "Apparently, she found out the week after you left on the assignment. She was waiting for you to come home to surprise you. When she told Drake after the funeral, he stepped in and married her so she'd be on his insurance. She'd already decided to return to Hazard, and he didn't want her to worry about anything. He knew if something happened, and the baby needed medical care, or Blair couldn't work, it would be harder to get him on the insurance policy after the fact, so Drake made sure they were both covered in advance."

Hadley blinked. "Him? I—I have a son?"

"Yeah. Trevor—cute kid. Smart as a whip."

He leaned back in the chair and pondered that for a few moments. "So . . . it was for the insurance only? They weren't . . . together?" He sounded hopeful as if there was a chance his former life could still be salvaged.

Shit, here comes the next bomb. At least Hadley was unarmed, so he couldn't shoot the messenger, no matter how much he would probably want to. "No, not at first . . . but down the road, I guess they fell for each other. They have two more kids now—a girl and another boy. Regan is three, and Michael just turned two."

His jaw clenched, and his eyes went blank before he

drank the rest of his scotch in two gulps. Standing, he dropped the glass on the coffee table with a *clunk* and headed for the door to the hallway and the elevator beyond. Carter stared after him. "Where are you going?"

"Doesn't fucking matter."

The Deimos operative sighed heavily, downed the remainder of his drink, and glanced at his watch. He had an hour before he was due to check in with his woman, Jordyn Alvarez, who was currently on an assignment in North Africa after assisting with Grant's rescue. She'd visited him for two days last week, but it felt like a month since then. Although they'd known each other for years, their boyfriend/girlfriend and Dominant/submissive relationships were relatively new.

Getting to his feet, he followed Hadley. The guy may not want company, but since he didn't have any ID or a dime in his pocket, it was Carter's duty to at least tail him and ensure he stayed out of trouble. Yeah, that was probably going to be easier said than done.

Chapter 2

Blair Hadley startled awake, her gaze sweeping the room as she tried to catch her breath. A sheen of perspiration coated her skin as her heart pounded in her chest. The early morning sun peeping around the edges of the curtains hanging over the windows gave her enough light to see where she was. It shouldn't surprise her that she was in the same bedroom she'd shared with Drake for the past six years in Hazard Falls, Kansas. It was where they'd consummated their marriage a full year after their courthouse nuptials. But her dream had been so real, so seemingly tangible, she'd expected to find herself in her old townhouse near Washington D.C.—the one she'd lived in with Grant for four years.

Turning onto her side, she found the other half of the bed empty, which wasn't unusual. Drake was an early riser, sometimes heading out to his studio, a converted barn behind their farmhouse, to work on his "latest masterpiece," as Blair called it. Others would see it as a custom-made piece of furniture. Her husband was talented and could turn fallen trees into stunning yet functional art. It had taken a few years for his reputation to grow to the point he'd been able to leave his job in construction and still support his family. Blair's income from translating novels from English to French for indie authors and a publishing company, Red Rose Books, had helped. It was a career she loved, satisfying her reading addiction and letting her work from home in between raising three young children. Now that Drake also worked from home, they split the child-rearing duties and housecleaning. After several hours of crafting furniture or the occasional commissioned sculpture, Drake would join his wife and kids for lunch before taking over for Blair so she could lock herself in her office and translate in peace.

After six years of marriage, though, she still thought of Grant. He'd been her first love and her first devastating heartache, other than losing both her parents within eight months of each other a few years before. But then Drake stepped in and cared for her after Grant's death. She hadn't expected him to propose to her, and at the time, she'd called him crazy, but once things had calmed down, she'd realized his idea had been a good one.

Blair couldn't stay in D.C. after Grant's death—honestly, they'd both been busy with their careers, so they really hadn't made many friends in the area. She'd had no one she was close to whom she could rely on as a grieving mother-to-be. She'd done some novel translations in her spare time, during the evenings and weekends when Grant had been out of the country, so she knew she could make a good living if she did it full-time. And with almost everything done via the internet nowadays, she could easily do it from anywhere in the world. However, a major drawback of leaving her job as a document translator at the French embassy would've been paying for her health insurance. Adding Trevor onto the policy after he was born would've almost doubled her monthly costs.

She'd never thought she'd fall in love again—hadn't wanted to after Grant had been ripped from her life—but as time passed, she and Drake had gotten close. She'd always thought he was just as attractive as Grant, and when her body had started to come alive again, whenever he was in the room, she'd thought it was one-sided. Then, one night, a few months after Trevor had been born, it'd been like someone had flipped a switch.

Five years earlier . . .

"Finally, he's asleep," Blair announced as she entered the kitchen, where Drake cleaned their dinner dishes. She grabbed a towel from where it had been hanging on the oven handle and took a saucepan from him to dry.

He smiled at her. "Guess the medicine is working. Maybe you can get some sleep now too."

They'd both been up since around 5:00 a.m. that morning with an inconsolable Trevor. He'd developed an ear infection and had been screaming his head off more than not. They'd taken him to his pediatrician's office as soon as it'd opened. The doctor had told them the medicated drops and antibiotics would work for now. Still, it was possible Trevor would eventually need tubes placed into his ears to avoid future occurrences. His ear canals were narrower than average for a baby his age. Having Trevor and her covered by Drake's insurance was just one of many reasons Blair was grateful for all his help. Without him, she'd be all alone, juggling her income versus her bills, in addition to working and caring for the infant.

While their marriage was unconsummated—they slept in separate bedrooms—they'd become close friends over the past year, more than ever before. Somewhere along the line, she'd stopped thinking of Drake as just the brother-in-law he would've been by this point or Grant's younger brother, and now he was Drake—her husband. The man she'd grown attracted to over the past few weeks, ever since her body had recovered from giving birth to a ten-and-a-half-pound baby that had required her to have an episiotomy. Yup, that hadn't been fun. But Drake had been there for her every step of the way. He'd read dozens of books and blogs on what to expect during her pregnancy and the first few years of Trevor's life. He'd never once complained about her invading his life and home, and she thought he'd had more fun than she had picking out furniture, toys, clothes, and other necessities for when the new baby arrived. It'd been a bittersweet moment when Trevor Grant Hadley had come into the world, looking so much like the biological father he'd never know. But Drake had stepped into the role without a moment's hesitation, and as he became the only father figure Trevor might ever have, he'd begun to crawl into Blair's heart and mind as well. Now, she found herself wondering what it would be like to kiss, touch, and make love to the man standing next to her.

The people in their small town had figured out Drake and Blair's marriage was one of convenience after she could no longer hide her pregnancy two months after their quickie wedding at the courthouse. Most of them had been supportive, but Blair had become the target of several single, jealous women who'd hoped to wrangle the good-looking former bachelor themselves. Part of their marriage agreement Blair had insisted on was that Drake would date other women if he felt like it, and he'd conceded by saying he'd be discreet if it ever happened. However, as far as she knew, he hadn't been with another woman since she'd moved into his home. Until recently, she'd felt contrite about putting such a damper on his dating life, but now that her attraction to him was growing, her own green-eyed monster didn't like to think of him being with another woman.

"Are you going to spend an hour drying that, or can I put it away?"

Startled, she glanced at his amused smile, then down at the counter. Everything else had been put away, and the sink had been drained. Sheepishly, she handed him the pan. "How long did I zone out for?"

He shrugged, then placed the pan into its proper cabinet. "A few minutes, but it's no big deal. I'm surprised you haven't crashed already. Between Trevor this morning and staying up late last night, finishing that translation you were working on, I'm surprised you're not asleep on your feet."

"Me, too, actually." She yawned and shook the growing cobwebs from her mind. "Is it wrong of me to hope he sleeps through the entire night for once?"

"Not at all." Moving closer, he took the towel from her hand and tossed it on the counter. "In fact, why don't you head to bed now? I'm going to watch some TV for a while and do some work online." While their jobs paid the bills, Drake had been trying to grow his side business by increasing his presence online. The new Drake Hadley Designs website Blair had helped him create was getting more and more traffic lately, and there was currently a three-month wait for the completion of a custom-made order.

"Sounds like a plan. Do you need anything from the market? I'm going grocery shopping in the morning."

"I'll leave a list on the table if I think of anything. Now go to bed."

Giving him a sassy salute, she did as ordered, or at least she tried to. Leaving him in the kitchen, she walked down the hallway to the master bedroom suite. When she'd first moved in, Drake had insisted she take it while he moved into one of the three other bedrooms in the house he and Grant had grown up in. She'd tried to argue with him, but he'd refused to take no for an answer. At least his room had an adjoining bath that was shared with Trevor's nursery.

Entering the bedroom, she flipped the wall light switch up, and nothing happened. She tried it again, and the room remained dark. The switch activated the overhead fan but not the light, and the bulb in her bedside lamp had died yesterday. Lightbulbs were on her shopping list for the morning, but that didn't help her now. "Shit."

"What's wrong?"

Blair let out a short scream and spun around, her heart pounding in her chest. She hadn't heard Drake come down the hallway behind her. She lightly smacked his upper arm. "Don't sneak up on me like that!"

He chuckled, the deep sound setting off goosebumps on her skin. "Sorry, I didn't mean to. I was going to get my laptop. What's wrong?"

"The bulb went out in the fan light." She flipped the switch up and down a few times again as if to prove it to him.

"Damn, woman, I never knew you were so hard on lightbulbs. You're not a serial bulb killer leading a double life, are you?"

His teasing made her laugh—something she'd rarely done for almost a year following Grant's death. But since Trevor was born, she no longer felt guilty about enjoying life again.

"No, I'm not. I'll just get one—"

"I'll steal one from—"

They'd both spoken and turned toward the living room simultaneously, bumping into each other. Blair's foot struck the doorjamb, tripping her, and Drake quickly grabbed her by the upper arms to prevent her from falling. But the momentum of both their movements sent them crashing into each other, chest to chest, pelvis to pelvis.

"Oh!" Blair threw her arms around Drake's neck as they stumbled together. Her back hit the wall as Drake's body pinned her against it. Finally, they both got their feet under them and stabilized.

Lifting her gaze, Blair's eyes met Drake's. The heat she saw there matched the warmth stirring in her core. Neither of them moved. Was she imagining things? Or was he . . . wait . . . something hard pressed against her belly. Something very masculine and hard. That answered the unfinished question in her mind—his body was reacting in a way that demanded hers do the same.

She zeroed in on his mouth and couldn't resist the temptation. Going up on her tiptoes, she brought their lips together. For a moment, Drake didn't respond, but that changed in a flash. His hands grasped either side of her head and held it at the angle he needed to devour her. His body was flush against hers as she ran her fingers through his hair. Their tongues danced, each one tasting the other. It wasn't long before they were both gasping for air.

Pulling back until he could study her face, Drake gulped. "Please . . . please, tell me you kissed me first, and it wasn't a figment of my imagination. If you did, I'm all for it and would love to do it again. But if you didn't, and I took advantage of the situation, then that makes me an asshole. Because—"

Her fingers covered his mouth. "I kissed you first, and I liked it . . . a lot."

He smiled under her hand and then grasped it with his own, moving it away so he could speak. "Thank God, because I've been wanting to kiss you for months and—"

Closing the distance between them, Blair didn't let him finish because she didn't want either one of them analyzing what they were doing just yet—not before she had a chance to taste him again. She felt like a desirable woman again for the first time in over a year.

Chapter 3

Present . . .

"Hey, Hadley! Wait up!"

Grant glanced over his shoulder and slowed his gait as his foreman, Rhys Buchanan, jogged toward him. It'd been a long day on the construction site, and he was looking forward to a three-day holiday weekend off with nothing to do but go fishing with a cooler full of beer in the Gulf of Mexico. The temperature in Tampa, Florida, had been tipping over the ninety-degree mark over the past week as Memorial Day approached.

He liked getting away from the loud city. Most people were able to tune it out. But after six years in a mountain-side prison camp, where the nighttime silence was almost as harsh as the beatings he'd endured, Grant found it difficult to tolerate the excessive noise sometimes. Hell, they'd made him dig a hole in the ground before throwing him into it and covering it with a sheet of metal held down by rocks. More than once, he'd thought they'd never come back and let him out, and the hole would become his grave. But his captors *always* came back for him, and then the interrogators would take another crack at him.

He hadn't been the only prisoner being held in the camp, but he *had* been the only American.

Stopping behind his gray Ram 1500 pickup truck, he dropped the tailgate and set his toolbox in the bed just as Buchanan caught up to him. Grant eyed the tall, blond-haired man. "What's up?"

"What are you doing tomorrow?"

He shrugged. "Planned on going fishing. Why?"

"Parker and Shelby are having a big barbecue, and she told me to invite you."

Rhys's amused grin told Grant all he needed to know. Parker Christiansen, the co-owner and founder of New Horizons, the construction company they worked for, was a really nice guy and took good care of his employees. His wife was a cute pixie of a woman who loved to play matchmaker for some of the single men who worked for her husband, and she was determined to hook Grant up with someone. For the past few months, he successfully dodged her attempts to set him up on blind dates, but the woman was a bulldog if she thought someone needed a significant other.

"In other words, she's invited some woman she thinks is perfect for me."

"Yup." His boss clapped him on the shoulder. "Don't take offense—it just means she likes you."

He leaned against the tailgate. "Yeah, I know. Any chance I can get out of it without hurting her feelings?" He really liked Shelby, despite her matchmaking efforts, and didn't want to insult her.

"Not unless you want her to get more devious. C'mon—show up for a few hours, flirt with the woman Shelby introduces you to, and maybe you'll find you both have some things in common. It'll be fun."

"Says the man already in a committed relationship," he replied dryly. While some of the guys they worked with had a problem with the rugged-looking foreman being gay and living with his architect boyfriend, Lincoln Perry, Grant didn't. Those who did wisely kept it mostly to themselves. New Horizons was an equal-opportunity employer, and any form of harassment, especially based on gender, race, or sexual orientation, was a reason to be canned—and the policy was strictly enforced. However, Grant heard a few jackasses talking behind Rhys's back a few months ago at a bar after work, using plenty of derogatory names to refer to the boss. One of them hadn't known when to shut his mouth and ended up with a black eye, bruised jaw, and sore ribs courtesy of the former CIA man. Since then, none of the bigots had said anything about Rhys, Linc, or anyone else they disliked in front of Grant, which was fine with him.

Sighing, he rolled his eyes. "Okay—what time? I'll brush up on my magic tricks."

Shelby and Parker adopted two adorable boys from Argentina last year. While they weren't blood brothers, they were both seven years old and had been best friends in an orphanage. They got a kick from the simple magic tricks Grant learned as a kid. His skills had improved as he'd gotten older, and some of the sleight-of-hand illusions had come in handy during his time with the CIA.

After deciding to remain "dead"—at least in the eyes of anyone who'd known him nearly eight years ago, with a scant few exceptions—he'd assumed a new life and relocated to Tampa. One of the people who knew about his past was Ian Sawyer—a retired Navy SEAL, the co-owner of a private security company with government contacts and high clearance, and a friend of Parker's. The man and his special-ops teams had been the ones who'd snuck into North Korea with Carter and rescued Grant. With Ian and Carter's help, Grant had started a new, low-key life in Florida twenty months ago. If his past ever came back to haunt him, he could count on Sawyer and his men to provide backup.

As far as his boss and coworkers knew, Grant had done a four-year stint in the Navy, where he'd supposedly met Sawyer, before opting out and going into construction. It hadn't been too difficult to fake since his father had worked in the blue-collar field, and Grant and Drake had spent their teenage summers working alongside him. The old man had passed away from a heart attack two years before Grant had been allegedly killed, and he was grateful. It would have destroyed Joseph Hadley if one of his sons had preceded him in death after raising them as a single father. Grant had been ten, two years older than Drake, when their mother, Susan, had died from complications during childbirth—her premature daughter had been stillborn. Joe and his young sons had been devastated but managed to continue their lives despite their loss.

"Any time after two. Parker said just bring yourself —food and drink are on the house."

"Sounds good. See you there."

Getting into his truck, Grant turned up the radio and the AC. He pulled out of the dirt parking lot and headed home for a shower. After that, he'd walk over to Donovan's, an Irish pub owned by the brother of one of the retired SEALs on Sawyer's team. It was only four blocks from his apartment, so he didn't have to worry about drinking too much and being unable to drive home. A few beers, a good dinner, a baseball game, and some mindless chatter with a few of the barflies would kill another few hours of the day. It wasn't like he had anything better to do.

Chapter 4

Grant woke up later than usual with the mother of all hangovers. A few beers had turned into shots of whiskey after a couple in their twenties had sat next to him at the bar. Everything had been fine until he heard the guy say his girlfriend's name—Blair. Of the hundreds of thousands of names in the world, why in hell had her parents named her Blair? And out of almost 400,000 people living in the city of Tampa, why did *those* two sit next to him? Contemplating his rotten luck and the memories they'd conjured up, he'd knocked back enough shots that Mike Donovan had insisted on driving him the short distance home.

After popping a few Tylenol caplets into his mouth, Grant threw on a pair of shorts, a T-shirt, and sneakers and took a two-mile run to sweat the last of the alcohol out of his system. He also did it to punish himself for getting that drunk.

Once he returned to his apartment, a shower and a greasy bacon, egg, and cheese sandwich had him feeling much better. One or two bottles of "hair of the dog" at the barbecue, and he'd be back to normal. Last night had been the first time he'd gotten falling-down drunk since the three-day bender he'd gone on after finding out Blair and Drake had gotten married. His brother had the family, complete with children, that Grant was supposed to have had.

Pushing the thoughts of the *happy couple* from his head, Grant parked behind a row of cars on the residential street the Christiansens lived on. Just as he turned off the engine, his cell phone chimed with an incoming text. His eyes narrowed as he grabbed the phone from the dash. He rarely got texts—hell, he rarely got phone calls. Maybe it was Mike checking to see if Grant was okay after last night.

The phone number on the log wasn't familiar, and he opened the text. His blood ran cold as the image registered in his mind. It was a picture of Blair, with a boy about six or seven years old, strolling down the sidewalk on Main Street in Hazard Falls. But the image had been altered. Someone had photoshopped in crosshairs, with Blair and the boy in the center. The boy . . . his son. Grant had never seen him before, even in photos—he'd resisted the urge to look up Blair or Drake on social media. But it had to be Trevor. His blond hair was the same shade as his mother's, and Grant would bet anything his eyes were blue too. But the rest of his facial features came from Grant. Right now, though, that didn't matter. Trevor was in danger, and so was Blair. The only reason someone would send the photo to him was they knew who Grant really was and they were threatening his family.

Scrambling from the truck, he ran up the street to Parker's house and through a gate in the fence leading to the backyard. Several people greeted him, but he ignored them, his gaze searching for the two men he needed. Spotting both Ian Sawyer and Carter sitting at a table with their women, he pushed through the small crowd of partygoers. The Deimos spy saw him coming and jumped to his feet. Grant could almost imagine what he looked like for Carter to go on alert like that. The man frowned. "What's wrong?"

With a shaking hand, Grant held out his phone with the image on the screen. Carter took it, cursed under his breath, and showed it to his girlfriend, Jordyn, and then Sawyer, who responded with his own muttered expletive. "Shit." The retired SEAL turned back toward the table. "Angel—Carter, Jordyn, and I have to take Grant to the compound. Do you want to stay here?"

As she held their new baby, his wife eyed Sawyer in confusion, but she seemed to know that was not the time to ask what was happening. "I'll stay. Kristen and Jenn will be here soon—one of them will drive me home."

"I'll leave you the SUV so we don't have to swap out the car seat." After kissing her and their baby goodbye, Sawyer slapped Grant on the shoulder. "Let's go. I'll call Egghead on the way and tell him to get his ass over there. He'll trace where this came from."

Without another word to anyone else and ignoring all the stares being sent their way, the three men and one woman left the party in a hurry. Grant knew Parker and Shelby wouldn't be surprised that some of their operative guests had to run out of there, but he was sure they were curious about why he was with them. However, he didn't care about anyone else but Blair and . . . and his son right now.

Thirty minutes later, they were in the war-room at the Trident Security offices. The computer setup could rival that at the CIA headquarters. Brody "Egghead" Evans grumbled about how the message had been bounced worldwide before landing in Grant's cell. "It wasn't actually sent from another phone. Whoever sent it used a texting service site and rerouted it through numerous servers. Give me a few more minutes, and I might be able to narrow it down."

At least the man was no longer complaining that his pregnant wife had to drop him off before going to the party without him, and there had better be some of her strawberry shortcake left by the time he got there.

Grant paced back and forth while the others worked. Jordyn was on another computer, checking out the chatter on the Dark Web. "So far, I can't find any mention of you, Blair, or Hazard Falls, but it could take hours or days to find a reference if it was coded."

In his office next door, Sawyer was on the phone with Lane Myers—a guy from Hazard Falls whom Grant had been a year ahead of in school. Myers had enlisted in the Marines, and his team worked alongside Sawyer's SEAL Team Four on several missions. After four tours, Myers returned to his hometown and went into law enforcement. While Sawyer wouldn't be too forthcoming, at first, with why he was inquiring about any strangers asking about Blair Hadley in the small town lately, Grant knew they would have to trust Myers with the truth. He hoped the guy could keep a secret. Grant would do anything to keep his family safe from his past, but he would do it covertly and with people he had faith in. Letting Blair and Drake know he was alive was a last resort—he just prayed it didn't come down to that.

DRAKE FINISHED STAINING THE SIX-FOOT DINING ROOM table he'd been working on. Tomorrow, he'd start adding several layers of varnish. In the meantime, he had eight chairs lined up on a platform, each waiting for their coats of cherry stain to dry. He was ahead of schedule with the pieces and would call the client on

Tuesday when he knew for certain the set could be delivered by next weekend. But for today, he was done working. After a shower, he and his family would head to a barbecue at the Red River Ranch.

The Triple-R was owned by Drake's longtime friend, Shane Wilson, his husband, Tucker, *and* their wife, Paige. Yup, the trio had a ménage marriage, as weird as that may sound to some people. Drake couldn't understand how a guy could share his woman with another guy, but it worked for them, and that was all that mattered. It probably helped that Shane and Tucker were in love with each other, in addition to loving their wife. That probably freaked out the bigots in town more than the ménage did. It wasn't the first shared marriage with a woman for the men either. Their first wife, Sarah, had died a little over three years ago, leaving behind the two widowers and a six-year-old daughter, Arianna. When Paige Merritt had been hired on as a house manager and the little girl's nanny, Shane and Tucker had fallen in love with her, and she with them. Now, they had a new baby to add to the mix —Ashley Sarah had gotten her middle name from Arianna's mother.

Using a rag and some turpentine, Drake scrubbed a few spots of stain that had gotten on his forearms, just above the rubber gloves he'd been wearing. Once that was done, he quickly surveyed his workspace and ensured everything was in order before closing up and heading toward the house. He'd almost reached the side porch when the family dog, a Labrador/border collie mix named Roscoe, began barking, alerting Drake to a white SUV coming down the driveway. The red and blue light bar on the roof made it easily recognizable as belonging to the police department.

Drake waited for the vehicle to stop and saw that Lane Myers was the driver. He strode over as the lawman climbed out and gave Roscoe an ear scratch. "Hey, Lane. What's up?"

The man wasn't wearing his usual working uniform of dark trousers and a white button-down shirt, with a loaded duty belt. Instead, he wore comfortable jeans, a T-shirt, and cowboy boots. He was still armed, but his handgun, shield, and cell phone were the only things attached to his belt. A pair of handcuffs was most likely at the small of his back.

Lane held out his hand to Drake. "Not much. Just checking out a report of a suspicious vehicle in the area. Have you seen anyone out of place?"

Strangers in a small town tended to stick out like a Great Dane in a pack of Chihuahuas. "Nope. Anything wrong?"

Lane seemed to hesitate a moment before answering. "Probably not. Just keep an eye out."

"Yeah, sure. You heading to the Triple-R?"

"I've got a few things I have to do first, but I'll be there later." Lane smiled for the first time since his arrival, although it didn't seem to go all the way to his eyes. "I'm looking forward to Lou turning me down for a dance."

Drake burst out laughing. Betty Lou Davidson and Lane had dated in high school, but something had happened between them, and Lane had gone off and joined the Marines. Since his return to Hazard Falls a few years ago, Lou had been trying to convince everyone, including herself, that she hated the man, but it was obvious she was fighting a losing battle. People all over town were placing bets on when she would finally cave—of course, they kept that fact from her, or they'd never get served in the restaurant she owned, Bar None. "You'll wear her down yet. I don't know why she doesn't just give up and admit she's into you."

"She will, someday. In the meantime, I'm enjoying the thrill of the chase."

Behind Drake, the screen door to the house opened, and he turned to make sure it wasn't little Michael trying to stage one of his famous escapes to play hide and seek. But it wasn't any of the kids—it was Blair, and she looked terrified. The blood had drained from her face. Her eyes were wide, and her mouth was opening and closing without any sound coming from her lips. Her entire body was shaking, and she looked like her knees were about to give out.

His stomach dropping, Drake ran to her side. "Blair! What's wrong?" He helped her to the rocking chair next to the door, and she collapsed onto it. Drake fell to his knees in front of her. "What is it, baby? Are the kids okay?"

He was about to stand again and run inside to search for his children when Blair's faint voice reached his ears. "L-look."

"What?" Confused, it took a second for his gaze to drop from her drawn face to her trembling hand. He grabbed the phone she held out to him and stared at the screen. Within seconds, he was as pale as she was. "Oh, my God."

"What is it?" Lane asked with concern. Drake hadn't even heard the man join them on the porch.

Trying to comprehend what he saw, Drake shook his head and showed Lane the image on the screen. "If I didn't know better, I'd swear that's Grant—my dead brother."

Chapter 5

Fourteen hours later . . .

Ian parked the rental car in front of the two-story farmhouse, next to a sheriff's department's SUV, and glanced around, noting a large pen with about a dozen chickens in a side yard. "Hazard Falls kind of reminds me of Bannerman's place in fucking Iowa. How people put up with roosters cock-a-doodling every morning is beyond me."

In the passenger seat, Carter snorted. "Nothing beats fresh eggs in the morning, dude. My sister has a bunch of chickens."

"Another reason why I'm staying away from Montana, besides the snow and sub-zero winters. Let's get this over with." Turning off the engine, he opened the door, climbed out, and met Carter by the hood. "God, this is going to fucking suck."

"It already sucks."

As they approached the front door, it opened, and Ian recognized the Marine he'd served a few tours with. "Myers, it's been a while."

The tall, brown-haired man stepped outside, letting the door close behind him, and held out his hand. "I wish it were under better circumstances, Sawyer. Good to see you, though. How are things in Tampa?"

"Good. No offense, but I want to wrap things up here pretty quickly. My wife just made me a father."

Lane grinned. "Well, damn. Didn't see that coming. Congrats."

"Thanks." He gestured between the two men. "This is T. Carter—don't ask what the T stands for. Carter, Lane Myers."

They shook hands, then Lane sighed heavily. "Look, Drake and Blair will take this really hard."

"What have you told them so far?" Carter asked.

"Very little. I said I called a few contacts I had in law enforcement back East, and someone familiar with Grant's service and death was coming here to talk to them. They keep going back and forth, saying maybe it's Grant or maybe someone who looks like him, but either way, they can't figure out why someone sent Blair the photo."

Ian frowned and ran a hand through his short, black hair. "Neither can we, but I guarantee, whatever the reason, it isn't good. Trust me, we'll do what we can to figure it all out and make sure your friends and Grant are safe." Yesterday, he'd arranged for two retired Navy SEALs and two retired MARSOC Raiders, who lived within driving distance of Hazard Falls, to keep an eye on the Hadley farm. As of twenty minutes ago, none of the men covertly hiding around the perimeter of the four-acre property had seen anything out of the ordinary. Ian and Carter also talked Grant out of not telling his family he was alive. Someone was forcing his hand, and like it or not, the man had to come clean and face his past.

"And Grant?" When neither of the other men immediately answered, Lane raised his eyebrows. "I'm not a small-town hick cop, Sawyer."

"Never said you were. Small town?" He looked to his left and then right. "Yeah, it doesn't get much smaller than this. But hick is definitely not a word I'd use for you—I've seen you in action. Now, if you want, I can come up with a new nickname for you—I've got a twat-roster I've been keeping, and I add to it all the time."

A knowing grin accompanied a shake of his head. "A twat-roster? No, thanks. I remember some of the nicknames you came up with in 'Stan—I'll pass." He paused. "So, where is he?"

"Nearby, waiting to make his grand entrance. I would've hired a band for the occasion but couldn't swing it on short notice." Ian nodded toward the house. "Are we ready?"

The corners of Lane's mouth dropped again as he nodded. "Yeah. Let's do it."

Turning on his heel, he led them into the house. "Their kids are with friends for the day—I thought it would be best they weren't around."

They followed him into a large, comfortable living room. A couple stood from where they'd been sitting on a couch. Ian recognized Blair Hadley from photos that had been sent to Grant. There was a slight family resemblance between Drake and his brother—it was in their facial structure. Drake was about two inches shorter than Grant but weighed about the same. His brown hair was a few shades lighter than Grant's, and instead of hazel, his eyes were the color of deep moss. Blair was a pretty woman with blue eyes and pale blonde hair that came to the top of her shoulders. She stood about five feet five, and her feminine curves were probably the result of her three pregnancies. They reminded Ian of the curves Angie had acquired while carrying his child—damn, how he loved them.

The couple's matching looks of confusion probably related to the fact that Ian and Carter were dressed in cargo pants and jeans, respectively, and black T-shirts. That, paired with Carter's long blond hair pulled back in a ponytail and the goatee Ian had sported for the past two weeks, made them look nothing like the well-kempt government agents the Hadleys had most likely expected.

A Border Collie mix sniffed both men before flopping down in the attached dining room as Lane intro-duced everyone. "Blair, Drake, this is an old military friend of mine, Ian Sawyer, and this is T. Carter."

As Drake shook both their hands, Blair's gaze bounced from one man to the other. It finally settled on Ian. "You're not with the Secret Service, are you?"

"No, ma'am," he responded, indicating for them to sit on the couch again while he claimed one of two leather recliners. Carter took the other one, and Lane remained standing. "I'm a retired Navy SEAL. I own a private security business that has classified govern-ment contracts." That was more than he usually told strangers, but it had a purpose today.

Her gaze shifted to Carter, who leaned forward, setting his elbows on his knees. "I work for the govern-ment, but not the Secret Service." He wouldn't say who he worked for but let them draw their own conclusions.

"I—I don't understand . . ."

Drake's eyes widened as he quickly figured it out. "Grant didn't work for the Secret Service, did he? He worked for the CIA. I always suspected—"

"*CIA?*" Blair looked even more confused. "What—what? How . . . what are you talking about?"

Carter let out a deep breath. "I'll tell you as much as I can, but please understand I might not be able to answer some of your questions—I might not be *allowed* to answer them. And what I do tell you today, cannot leave this room."

"So, you're CIA too?" Drake asked.

"No, I'm not, but I occasionally work with their agents. That's how I knew Grant—we often crossed paths in Asia and the Middle East. As you can imagine, his ability to speak several languages made him a huge asset to the government."

A small smile appeared on Drake's face. "He was always good with foreign languages—how he picked them up so easily when I could barely pass Spanish 101 was always a joke between us."

Carter nodded and continued. "Right before he disappeared, he was undercover in Asia—I'm sorry, but I can't be more specific than that—and his cover was blown. We're not sure how. I was the closest US operative to his last known location, so I scrambled to try to find and extricate him. Again, I can't give you many details, but I found out he was abducted and taken out on a boat. When I tried to catch up to them, I saw them toss a body overboard, tied with heavy weights. I was on my own, and by the time I could get to the spot, the body had disappeared. The trench was far too deep for me to recover it, even if I had SCUBA gear with me—which I didn't." He swallowed hard. "Please understand, I did everything I could to confirm or refute that it was Grant. The resulting investigation made the CIA ninety-nine percent sure it was him."

"But it wasn't him, was it?" Blair's lips trembled as a tear rolled down her pale cheek. Drake put his arm around her shoulders and pulled her closer.

Carter's voice was filled with remorse. "No, it wasn't. It was a ruse, in case anyone was watching—they probably swapped Grant with some homeless guy or someone who wouldn't be reported missing. It was over six years before we discovered the truth. We discovered through a CIA contact that Grant was being held in a prison camp. With the help of Ian's teams, we went in and pulled him out."

"Oh, my God. He—he's really alive?" She pointed to a cell phone sitting on the coffee table with a trembling hand. "That's real-really him in that photograph?"

Standing, Ian gestured to the phone. "May I?"

Drake nodded and picked up the device. He entered a code and then handed it to Ian. The photo on the screen was definitely Grant. Ian could tell it was taken recently because Grant stood in front of a commercial construction site Parker's company had just started working on. He showed the photo to Carter. "That was taken no more than two weeks ago."

"When did you rescue him? And where has he been since then? Why weren't we told before now?" The questions rushed from Blair's mouth as more tears flowed.

Carter grimaced. "Almost two years ago. He recovered at a military hospital in Germany for the first few weeks. Since then, he's lived in Tampa, Florida, working in construction for a friend of ours."

Stunned, Drake repeated his wife's last question. "Why weren't we told before now?"

"That was Grant's decision. At first, he hadn't wanted anyone to see him in that condition—emaciated—but then . . ." The covert operative didn't finish his sentence, clearly letting the couple figure it out.

Grant's brother blanched. "Oh, God. He found out Blair and I were married, didn't he?"

"Yeah. When he was finally well enough, he asked about Blair. I had to tell him the truth—it would've been worse if he found out on his own. I told him about your wedding and your kids. He knows Trevor is his too. Grant thought it was best if you weren't told."

Drake jumped to his feet, his anger taking hold. "Best! Best for fucking who? I don't believe this! I—"

"Drake, calm down," Lane said. "Just calm down. I know this is hard on both of you, but it's got to be hard on him too."

"I'm not saying what he did was right or wrong, but please, think about it from his point of view," Carter added, sympathy and understanding in his tone. "The woman he loved and planned to spend the rest of his life with thought he was dead. She's now married to his brother, and they have three kids. He told me that, for six years, Blair was the reason he fought to stay alive. At the time he made the decision not to tell you, he wasn't strong enough to see the two of you together—to see the life he could have had. It took him months to recover from what he'd gone through."

A shuddering sob ripped from Blair's chest, and her husband sat next to her again, pulling her into his arms. The other men gave the couple a few minutes to compose themselves. Finally, Blair looked at Carter with wet, bloodshot eyes. "How did you know all of that about us? How did you know about Trevor?"

"I had someone keep an eye on you," the spy confessed. "Out of guilt, I guess. For years, I felt I'd failed Grant—I hadn't been able to save him. To atone for it, I wanted to ensure you were okay."

"You had someone watching me? Us?"

She glared accusingly at Lane, who held up his hands in defense. "It wasn't me, Blair. While I've known Ian since I was in the Marines, I just met Carter today. And I only found out Grant was alive after you received the photo."

"It wasn't Lane," Carter confirmed. "It wasn't anyone who lives in Hazard Falls. A retired operative lives nearby in Garden City. It wasn't hard for him to find out how you were doing. It's a small town—people talk and don't always check to see who's eavesdropping. He wasn't watching you for all those years—just in the beginning, and then I had him get me an update after we landed in Germany and got Grant into the hospital. I knew he would ask questions, and I needed to know what to tell him."

"Around the same time you received that photo . . ." Ian interrupted, putting the conversation back on track and pointing to the phone he'd put back on the table, ". . . Grant received one of you and Trevor." Pulling out his own phone, he brought up the image

Brody had forwarded to him and showed it to the couple.

"That was last week," Blair said as she stared at the photo in shock. "We'd just left the dentist's office and were walking to the Stop & Go to get a few groceries. Who took that, and why did they send it to . . . to Gr-Grant? Oh, my God, he's alive!"

She buried her head in Drake's shoulder again as he looked at Ian. The retired SEAL shrugged. "We don't know who sent it or what their motive is. That's why we're here. We believe someone from Grant's past found out he's alive, and it looks like they know Trevor is his son, but beyond that, we have no idea what's going on."

"So, he sent you to talk to us? He didn't bother to come here himself?" Drake asked, his eyes flaring in anger once more.

"No, he's here—in Hazard Falls. He came to us for help after he got the photo. He was coming here, regardless, to watch over you himself, covertly, but once he found out you'd gotten the photo of him, he knew he would have to let you know he was alive. We thought it was best to lay the groundwork before he showed up out of the blue. I'm supposed to call him when you're ready to see him."

The couple stared at him a moment before looking at each other. They seemed to communicate without speaking. Finally, Drake nodded. "We're ready."

Chapter 6

Grant nervously tapped on the steering wheel of the second car Ian had rented as Jordyn sat in the passenger seat. Carter's woman was also a spy with Deimos, but Grant had never met her until his rescue. A talented sniper, she'd taken out several of his captors before they knew what was happening. Grant would've preferred torturing the bastards, as they'd done to him over the years, but getting out of there alive had been more important than revenge.

Ian and Carter had been at the home the Hadley boys had grown up in for almost an hour now, and the suspense was killing Grant. Following the death of their father, Drake had continued living in the house, commuting to his construction jobs and working on his side business of handcrafted furniture, which had still been in its infancy. After discussing things with

Grant, Drake had planned to eventually buy him out of the property they'd both inherited. At the time, Grant thought he'd be spending the rest of his life in the outskirts of D.C., where he and Blair had planned to settle down. In the months leading up to his capture, he'd seriously considered taking a stateside position with the CIA or switching teams and signing on with the Secret Service. The latter would've been simpler, considering Blair had thought that was who he worked for anyway. With agents assigned to visiting foreign diplomats all the time, the five languages he spoke—English, Spanish, Korean, Mandarin Chinese, and French—would've had him in high demand.

Jordyn's phone must have vibrated because she pulled it out from where she'd tucked it under her thigh and swiped the screen. "Hi, babe." She glanced at Grant. "We'll be there in a minute if he doesn't crash the car—his nerves are strung so tight he's ready to pop a vein bulging at his temple." A smile crossed her face. "Yeah, the same one Ian gets when he's ready to blow a gasket. See you in a minute."

As she disconnected the call, Grant took a deep breath, let it out, and then put the car in gear. Jordyn had been right; it only took a minute to drive up the road from where they'd been parked out of sight from anyone passing by and turn into the driveway leading up to the house where he'd spent his childhood. He stared at it as he pulled in next to the other rental. It looked so familiar yet so different. The old gray siding had been replaced by a soft beige. The porch and trim seemed to have gotten a new coat of white paint recently. Flower beds around the perimeter of the porch were in full bloom with reds, whites, pinks, and purples—something Grant hadn't seen since his mother had been alive. An American flag hung from a pole attached to one of the porch columns holding up its roof.

As he climbed from the vehicle, Grant's gut was in knots. The last time he'd ever felt this nervous was the first time he'd kissed Blair at the beginning of their junior year in high school. It'd been during a pep rally for the varsity football team as they prepared to play against their biggest rivals. Grant had fallen for the blonde-haired beauty he'd first met in French class during their freshman year. It'd taken him another two years and dating a few other girls before he'd finally worked up the courage to ask Blair out. Their relationship had survived them going to different colleges, him on a full scholarship to Georgetown University and her to the University of Kansas, her father's alumni. After they'd both graduated, she'd joined him in D.C. and was hired by the French embassy to translate nongovernmental documents and correspondence.

During his senior year in college, Grant applied for the Secret Service, thinking that being multilingual would give him an edge over other candidates during the hiring process. However, two weeks later, he'd been approached by a CIA recruiting agent. After having lunch with the woman, Grant was intrigued. Then, the more he thought about it, the more he believed he could do the job. He'd signed on at twenty-two and spent the next two years training to be a spy for the US before starting fieldwork. Besides being out of the country a lot, one of the few drawbacks was that he hadn't been able to tell his family or Blair what he truly did for the government. At the time, he hadn't thought it would be that big of a deal. Now, he knew how wrong he'd been.

As he stood there, staring at the closed front door, Jordyn came around the back of the vehicle and stopped beside him. She put a reassuring hand on his arm. "At first, it's going to be rough . . . for all of you. Just remember, no matter how tempers may flare up, deep down, I'm sure they're happy you're alive."

"And they hate me for not telling them that before now."

Sighing, she cocked her head toward the front door. "It'll be okay. Let's get this over with so we can find out who wanted them to know you're not six feet under. I don't like you standing out here in the open."

He didn't like it either, despite knowing several of Ian's contacts were watching the property. There couldn't be a good reason why someone had taken those photos and sent them to him and Blair. Since very few people knew he was alive, it was a fair bet it was his past coming back to bite him in the ass.

Forcing himself to walk toward the five steps

leading up to the front porch and door, he steeled himself against seeing the woman he still loved for the first time in about eight years. After seeing several pictures of her on social media, which he'd avoided like the plague until yesterday, he thought she was even more beautiful now, with the curves that had come from motherhood. But she wasn't his woman anymore —she was Drake's. And, once again, the thought tore at his gut.

As he reached the top of the stairs, the interior door swung open, revealing Carter. The man pushed open the screen door and let them enter. "In the living room."

Three more steps were all it took for his past and his present to collide. His gaze immediately landed on Blair and Drake, who sat beside each other on the couch. Blair gasped the moment she saw him, her entire body trembling as new tears flowed from her already swollen, red eyes. Meanwhile, Drake stared at Grant as if he couldn't comprehend that his brother was really standing there after all this time. Seconds passed—everyone remained quiet. The only sound was the ticking of the old grandfather clock, passed down through three generations of Hadleys, from where it stood in the corner of the room.

Grant couldn't find his voice, his gaze locked onto where Drake clutched Blair's hand. His brother squeezed it, then let go and stood. He circled around the side of the coffee table. Grant couldn't read his expression. When Drake stopped in front of him, Grant only had a split-second to see rage flare in his brother's eyes before a punch was thrown.

Blair's voice rang out, "Drake! Don't!"

No one else said a word or moved to interfere. This was between the two brothers.

Grant welcomed the pain that bloomed in his jaw as he stepped to the side to regain his balance. His hands went up in an automatic defensive gesture. He'd give Drake the one shot, but that was it. He'd deserved it for not telling them he was alive, but he also had anger simmering just below the surface. If Blair's and Trevor's lives weren't in danger, this would be a different reunion. Hell, there wouldn't have even *been* a reunion.

Shifting his jaw, he ran his tongue along his teeth to ensure none were loose as he glared at Drake. "Feel better?"

Drake snorted. "No—I don't know what I feel. I don't know what I'm *supposed* to feel. How—how could you not tell us you were alive, you bastard? It's been *years*—what feels like a fucking lifetime—and there wasn't a day that went by that I didn't think of you. Hell, even after all this time, there are days when I wished I could call you to ask for your input on some stupid matter—it didn't make a difference what it was —but then I remember I couldn't. How could you let us continue to believe you were dead?" His face reddened.

"You're my fucking brother, for God's sake! My flesh and blood!"

His gaze flickered to Blair and then back to Drake. "I'm sorry. Believe me when I say it was the hardest decision I've ever made. I couldn't . . . I just . . ."

Tears began to roll down their cheeks as if someone had turned on a faucet connected to the two men. Drake closed the distance between them and threw his arms around Grant, who did the same. He could feel the sobs the younger man worked hard to keep quiet while trying to keep his own in check. A minute or two passed before Drake took a shuddering breath, then stepped back, wiping his eyes with his hands.

At some point, Blair had stood and approached them. She seemed hesitant about moving any closer to Grant. Trying to encourage her to take the last few steps to him —he didn't want to overwhelm her more than he already had—he held out his hand. She stared at it momentarily, then slowly lifted a quivering hand and placed it in his. The moment they touched, she let out another gasp, and then suddenly, she was in his arms. He'd been dreaming of this since the day he'd been captured. All he'd wanted was one more minute to be this close to her. One more hour taking in her beauty. Just one more day making love with his sweet Blair before he died. As days had turned into weeks, weeks into months, months into years, he never thought he'd hold her again, much less see her.

Now, he held on for dear life, knowing when he let

go, it would never happen again. She was Drake's wife, which made Grant her brother-in-law. He didn't know how the hell he would get through the next few days until they figured out who'd manipulated this unplanned reunion. When they did, and after eliminating the threat against Blair and Trevor, Grant would graciously bow out of their lives and return to Florida. Maybe when he got there, he'd drink himself to death.

THREE HOURS LATER, GRANT HAD CONVINCED IAN, Carter, and Jordyn they could leave Hazard Falls—the four special-ops guys, who'd been watching over the family, would stick around until they were no longer needed. Ian had a wife and a new baby waiting for him at home, and Carter and Jordyn probably had to go out and save the world once more. A small part of Grant missed the call of duty, but that was his past. After he put an end to the person stalking him and his family, Grant would go back to being a blue-collar worker in Tampa who drank Budweiser while watching the various sports and history channels. Maybe he'd get a dog—at least that would give him a reason to get up every morning on his days off from work. During the week, he could bring it with him to work—a few of the guys brought their dogs to the sites. One of the first things they erected at each job site was a fenced-in run in the shade where the three big dogs could get fresh air and play without getting into trouble.

Yeah, a nice, big, badass pit bull with a heart of gold would be great. Grant silently vowed to visit an animal shelter when he got home to find the perfect companion to keep his mind off the fact his brother was married to the woman he loved. Not that he honestly thought it would work because, yup, he still loved her, even after all those years apart. Even after finding out she was in love with Drake. Not that Grant would ever admit that to anyone but himself.

Sitting with Lane, Drake, and Blair in the country kitchen he'd grown up in, Grant eyed the updates that'd been made since he'd last been there. Appliances had been upgraded to more modern models, the old cracked tile on the floor had been replaced with wood, and the 1970s flower wallpaper had been removed, making way for a bright yellow shade of paint. Beautiful new cabinets had been installed, and Grant guessed Drake had made them by hand. He'd always been talented when it came to woodwork.

Blair disconnected a call on her cell phone and set it on the kitchen table. "That was Danielle—she's bringing the kids home." Her gaze shifted to Grant, and he saw a pound of guilt in her eyes. "Trevor doesn't know you're his father. He's too young to understand." She hesitated before adding, "Maybe when he's older . . ."

Although they'd never met, it grated on him that his own son would be calling him "Uncle Grant," but Blair was right—Trevor was far too young to understand what'd happened. Hell, Grant was still having a difficult time with it, and he wasn't a little kid.

He nodded. "It's okay—I understand."

Relief pushed away some of the guilt in Blair's eyes, but not completely. Part of Grant felt bad for her—this had to be so hard for her—but the other half tried to convince him her guilty feelings were justified. Unfortunately, he had no one else to blame for her falling into Drake's arms besides himself and the North Koreans. Grant had selfishly signed up with the CIA, not thinking for one moment a mission would go to hell in a handbasket. He'd been young and cocky, certain he was invincible and could outsmart the enemy before returning to his alter-ego life with Blair. He'd been a bastard to lie to her and then put her through his presumed death. He deserved everything that'd happened back here in the States while he'd been held captive. So why couldn't he keep his gaze off her?

Lane cleared his throat and stood. "I should get going. Grant, I think it's best to bring in a few friends we can trust. I have no doubt Sawyer's men are good at what they do, but they're not from Hazard. Locals will have a better chance of noticing anyone out of place."

"Who do you have in mind?" Drake asked.

"Shane, Tuck, Hank, Seth, Tad, and the chief, for now. Maybe Lou, too—she can keep an eye out for any strangers walking into Bar None." Grant remembered Betty Lou Davidson—she and Lane had dated in high school. Her father owned the bar, or at least he had when Grant had lived in Hazard. Some of the others Lane had mentioned were familiar to him, although he only vaguely recalled Tucker Jones and Seth Parker. They worked for Shane Wilson at the Red River Ranch, otherwise known as the Triple-R. Hank Mathers also worked for Shane, but he'd been in Grant's high school class, and they'd both played on the varsity baseball team. Grant had no idea who Tad was, but apparently, everyone else did.

"That's an awful lot of people," Grant replied.

"And I trust every one of them." The statement had been said in a matter-of-fact tone, but there had also been a bit of a challenge.

He thought about it for a moment. The man was right. Things had changed since Grant had last been in Hazard Falls—a slight population boom had occurred. When he'd lived there, the population had been around 3000, but according to Google, about 800 more had been added to the census. Some people had moved away, while others had found a new life in the small town—he would be a stranger to some of the residents. An outsider. And until he knew who'd targeted Blair and Trevor, he needed all the help he could get. "All right."

Drake had gotten to his feet and was leaning against the kitchen counter. "Tell everyone to come here at seven tonight. We'll have to fill them in, and I'm sure they'll be as shocked as we were that Grant's alive. It's probably best to hit them with that here."

Lane nodded. "I'll make the arrangements. Call me if there's any trouble."

Turning on his heel, the lawman headed for the front door, leaving an awkward silence in his wake.

And then there were three.

Taking a deep breath, Grant stood. "Is the Moody Moon Motel still open? I'll get a room there."

"No!" Who was more surprised at Blair's barked word wasn't clear—her, Grant, or Drake. She glanced between the two men. "I mean, that's . . . that's not necessary. There's . . . um . . . there's a finished apartment over Drake's workshop. We rented it out for a while, but nobody's living there now. It's furnished and has whatever you . . . um . . . need. R-right, Drake?"

"Uh . . . yeah. Of—of course." He gestured toward the back door. "Blair's right. There's no reason you can't stay there, and you'll be close enough if this asshole shows up."

Grant stared at Drake a moment and then at Blair. They both still appeared shell-shocked about him coming back from the dead, so to speak, which wasn't unexpected. Maybe he should accept the offered room and go settle in to give them some time to recover, although, if he had better sense, he'd get a room at the motel. But, this way, he could keep a closer eye on Blair and Trevor—at least, that was what he told himself why he said yes. "Okay, sounds good. I'll just grab my bag from the car, then I'll take a look around and contact Sawyer's men again to make sure all is well."

He started for the front door but stopped when Blair called his name. He looked back over his shoulder at her. She brought her hand to her trembling lips. "I'm . . . I'm happy you're alive. I can't imagine what you . . ." She gulped. ". . . what you went through. I'm glad you're okay. It's just going to take some time to . . . to get used to it."

Grant pursed his lips, hesitated, then nodded. Unable to think of anything that didn't sound trite, he mutely left to get his bags. Surviving the emotional aspects of the next few days might be harder than anything else they would face.

Chapter 7

Holding an old photo of Grant and Drake, Blair sat at the kitchen table next to Trevor while her husband put Regan and Michael down for naps. They'd both been exhausted after coming home from Blair's friend's house, where they'd gone swimming with Danielle Harrison's sixteen-year-old twin girls, who'd babysat for a few hours. Zoe and Lily were Blair's go-to sitters whenever she and Drake took a rare night out without the children.

Trevor nibbled on the apple slices Blair had given him for a snack as she tried to come up with the words to explain Grant's return in a way his almost seven-year-old mind could understand.

Reaching out, she stroked his head and showed him the framed picture she'd taken from the wall in the family room. It'd been taken the summer before Grant and Blair had left for D.C. "Honey, do you remember what I told you about Daddy's brother, Grant?"

Trevor nodded. "Uh-huh. You said Uncle Grant was in heaven with our grandmas and grandpas."

"That's right, I did." She inhaled deeply and let it out slowly. "Well, Daddy and I found out today that we made a mistake. We . . . um . . . you see, um . . . we thought Grant had died in an accident, but the people who told us that were wrong. Sometimes, adults make mistakes, and this was one of them. Your Uncle Grant is alive, and . . . um . . . he came home to . . . uh, see us. He's here."

The little boy's eyes widened. "He is? Where? Can I see him?"

Her lips quivered as she tried to smile. "Of course, you can. In a little bit. He's . . . um . . . in the apartment over Daddy's workshop, taking a nap." Honestly, she didn't know what Grant was doing right now, but it really didn't matter for this conversation.

"Cool. So, is he going to live here with us?"

"No—no, sweetie. I mean, I don't know. For now, he's just visiting. He lives in Florida."

"Oh." He thought about that for a moment, then grinned. "Does that mean we can visit *him* someday and go to Disney World?"

She relaxed a little and chuckled. Ever since a friend from second grade told him about a trip to the Orlando theme park, he'd been begging to go. She was sure it would be on the Christmas list he would send to Santa later this year. "We'll see. For now, he'll be visiting us for a bit." A thought occurred to her. "Trevor, have any strangers approached you and tried to talk to you about me, Daddy, or Uncle Grant? Or have any strangers tried to talk to you at all?"

His little shoulders went up in a shrug as he chewed and swallowed the last piece of the apple. "Nope. I know I'm not supposed to talk to any adults I don't know, and I won't go with anyone who doesn't say the magic phrase."

The "magic phrase" they'd all agreed on was "Mr. Hippopotamus sent me," since the stuffed animal was Trevor's favorite when he was younger before passing it on to Regan, who'd recently given it to Michael. If a stranger tried to say Blair or Drake sent them to pick up their sons or daughter and didn't say that phrase, the children should yell "fire" as loud as they could and run. They were to tell anyone who responded to their alarm that the stranger wasn't their parent. Every few weeks, Blair made sure her children remembered the phrase and that it superseded any puppies, kittens, or candy a stranger might use to lure them away.

"Good boy." She got to her feet and ruffled Trevor's hair. "I have a few things to do before dinner. I'm making chicken tonight—do you want carrots or peas?"

"Peas, please. Can I go practice my pitching?" For his birthday, they'd gotten him a pitch-back rebounder. When he threw a baseball at it, the equipment's taut netting sent the ball flying back to him. It was a way to play catch by himself if no one else was around.

"Sure, just stay where Daddy and I can see you."

"'Kay."

The alarm on the clothes dryer buzzed, and Blair hurried to get the laundry out. After folding several towels, she went to the linen closet and got a set of spare sheets. Summoning up her courage to see Grant again, she strode out the backdoor, across the small lawn separating the house from the barn, and then took the stairs on the side of the building to the one-bedroom apartment. She knocked and waited for an answer as her stomach roiled in a combination of dread and anticipation. Hearing nothing, she turned to leave when the door swung open. Her heart nearly stopped, and her jaw went slack as she stared at Grant. God, he was still as handsome as ever. He hadn't shaved in a day or two, but she would know those sharp hazel eyes, firm jaw, and beautiful lips anywhere. What she wouldn't have given all those years ago to have one more hour with him.

Her heart was breaking in two. Here was who she'd thought she'd be spending the rest of her life with, while inside the house was the other man she'd fallen in love with in the first man's absence. She'd cursed the universe when it had taken Grant away from her, and her emotions were now all jumbled after he'd been returned to her nearly eight years later. She honestly didn't know which event was crueler. Had he kept the fact that he was alive a secret because he hated her and Drake and felt betrayed because they'd fallen in love with each other? It was a question she wasn't sure she wanted to hear the answer to.

"Blair?"

She blinked, unaware of how long she'd stood there, gaping at him. Shaking the torrent of emotional thoughts from her mind, she held out the stack of laundry to him. "You'll need new sheets and towels."

He took them from her. "Thanks." After a moment's pause, he stepped back and opened the door wider. "Want to come in?" When she hesitated, he added, "I won't bite, Blair."

Nodding, she swallowed hard, then stepped forward. When the door closed behind her, a feeling of being trapped flashed through her, but when she looked up into Grant's face, she saw his own anguish over the situation. This was killing him as much as it was her.

She tore her gaze from his and glanced around the sparse room filled with mostly necessities and very little décor. It'd been months since she'd been up there, and the apartment needed a good dusting and vacuuming. Through a partially opened door, she saw the stripped queen-sized bed. "Here, let me make the bed for you."

When she tried to take the sheets back from him, he moved them out of her reach and set them on a small table next to the room's couch. "I'll do it later. You don't need to cater to me, Blair."

She fidgeted, uncertain of what to do or say next. "Sorry."

"About what? About marrying my brother?" She gasped and paled at the words he'd viciously spit out as he ran a hand down his face. His tone and expression softened. "Shit, don't answer that. I'm sorry, Blair—that was completely uncalled for. I thought I'd gotten used to the idea and had accepted it, but . . . I guess not. The only person here to blame for this whole mess is me. None of this would have happened if I hadn't thought I was invincible back then. But it did, and nothing I can do will change that. I'm the one who's sorry—the last thing I'd ever wanted to do was hurt you."

"Grant, I never meant to fall in love with Drake, and it didn't happen right away. I grieved for you for over a year, and he was there for me—platonically." Hot tears scorched the skin on her cheeks. "I didn't even have a grave where I could visit you. If I did, I probably would've curled up into a ball and cried on it every day. I kept praying it was all a mistake. But after Trevor was born, I . . . I started to move on—it was time. I took one look at his sweet baby face, and suddenly, I had something to live for again. Up until that point, I'd just been going through the motions. I'm sorry nothing turned out like you and I planned, but how can I regret anything that's happened over the past seven years when it would mean I wouldn't have

Regan and Michael too? I love them as much as I love Trevor. And . . . and I love Drake now as much as I loved you then."

Not waiting for a response, she spun on her heel and ran out the door and down the stairs, swiping at the tears that wouldn't stop pouring forth. Once again, she cursed the universe, but this time, she didn't know the reason why.

DRAKE'S HAND PAUSED ON THE KNOB OF THE BACKDOOR as he stared outside the window. He watched as Grant approached Trevor, squatted in front of him, and held out his hand, which the little boy shook. Drake's gut churned. He'd always seen the resemblance between Trevor and the memories of Grant, his biological father, but never had it been more prominent now that the two were mere inches apart as they spoke. Grant said something that made Trevor smile and laugh. The boy nodded, glanced around, and then ran over to where the pitch-back was set up in the yard. He picked up Drake's baseball glove and gave it to Grant, who slid it onto his hand.

After putting some distance between them, Trevor threw the ball to Grant, who easily caught it. Back and forth, the ball was tossed as a lump formed in Drake's throat. God, he was jealous of his own brother, who was playing catch with his biological son!

What the hell is wrong with me? How many times have I wished Grant could see what an amazing kid Trevor is and how I regretted the boy would never know his real father?

No matter how he tried to convince himself he should be rejoicing over the fact his brother was alive, Drake couldn't shake the feeling that his family was about to be ripped from his arms. He couldn't step back and surrender Blair to the man she'd loved first. It may have taken time for them to consummate their marriage, but he was madly, passionately in love with his wife. They had a happy life in Hazard Falls and a beautiful family, and Drake would be damned if he gave that up—for anyone.

Drake heard Blair approach from behind, and he turned around. She had Michael in her arms, and Regan ran toward him. "Daddy!"

He bent down and picked her up. "Hey, there, my ray of sunshine. How was your nap?"

"Good!" She looked over his shoulder to where her older brother was still playing catch. "Who's that?"

He took a deep breath and stared at Blair. "That . . . that's your Uncle Grant." At least he could say that truthfully to his two youngest children. "Would you like to meet him?"

"Yes!" She and Michael were too young to know about Grant's alleged death. To them, he was just a man in some photos in various places around the house.

Putting her back down, he took Michael from Blair —the boy was still rubbing the sleep from his eyes. Blair gave Drake a weak smile and patted his arm. "Go introduce them. I better get dinner started if we're going to be done in time for the meeting."

Lane had texted Drake about an hour after he'd left and said he'd spoken to everyone on his list, and they'd all be there at 7:00 p.m. except for Betty Lou. One of her bartenders was sick, and she had no one but herself available to take his evening shift. Lane would fill her in on the details tomorrow if she were in the mood to speak to him at all.

"Are you okay?" he asked his wife. She'd been crying again but tried to hide the fact by taking a shower, where the children couldn't see her. However, her eyes were still red and puffy.

Her mouth thinned. "Not really, but I will be. It's just a lot to take in—Grant being alive, and someone taking that photo . . ." She glanced down, and Drake's gaze followed. Regan was staring up at both of them, listening intently. Blair pasted on a fake smile. "But we'll talk about that later. Go on outside, and let me get dinner started.

"Let's go, Daddy." Regan opened the interior and screen doors, and Drake followed her outside. Without waiting for him, she rushed to where Grant caught another throw. She stopped next to him, looked up, and waved cheerfully. "Hi! I'm Regan!"

Grant bent his knees and dropped to her level,

holding out his hand. "Well, hello there, Regan. I'm your Uncle Grant. It's nice to meet you."

She placed her tiny hand in his big one. "It's nice to meet you too. I'm five—how old are you?"

"Regan, you know it's not polite to ask adults that question," Drake admonished as he approached. His daughter was inquisitive to a fault sometimes.

She shrugged. "Sorry, I forgot."

Grant gently touched her cheek. "That's okay. Sometimes I forget it's not polite to ask certain questions too." Rising again, he faced Drake and studied the little boy in his arms. "And this must be Michael. God, he's the spitting image of you when you were that age."

"In the workshop, I have side-by-side photos of him and me as two-year-olds—it's freaking scary." Although things were tense between them, both men did a good job of hiding it from the children.

Michael squirmed in his arms. "Down, Daddy."

Drake did as his youngest ordered and set him on the ground. The boy squatted, picked up a rock, and examined it. They fascinated him, and Drake swore the kid would grow up to be a geologist or something along those lines.

"Hey, Dad," Trevor called out as he tossed the ball in the air and caught it. "Uncle Grant goes to the Royals games when they play the Rays in Florida." Watching the Royals' games on TV was something Trevor and Drake enjoyed doing together over the past two years. Even at such a young age, the boy could rattle off the starting lineup and got annoyed if a favorite player wasn't on it for any given game.

"Really? That's awesome." Drake ground his teeth together as he glared at Grant. It was sinking in that Grant had been enjoying life in Florida while everyone in Hazard Falls, Kansas, had thought he was dead. Drake also didn't miss his older brother's wince when Trevor had called him "Uncle Grant." Well, too bad—that was Grant's problem. If he hadn't been working for the CIA, Trevor would be calling *him* dad right now. Someday, they'd have to tell Trevor the truth, but Drake didn't even want to think about that at the moment because he had no idea how the hell they'd explain it to him.

That awkward silence returned between the two men as the children talked and played around them. Finally, Grant broke eye contact and gestured toward Trevor. "He's a great kid . . . they all seem to be. You and Blair have done a great job raising them."

"Someone had to." Shit, he hadn't meant to say that, but it was the truth.

Grant just nodded, his gaze on the ground as he toed the dirt in front of his foot. "Yeah, someone did . . . because I screwed up."

Drake looked away for a moment, and then his curiosity got the better of him. "What happened? I mean, how did you get caught?"

"I wish I knew. I—"

"Here, Uncle Grant. I picked you some flowers."

Both men's gazes dropped to the little girl who held a small bouquet of her mother's daisies.

Taking them from her, Grant smiled. "They're as pretty as you are, Regan. Thank you."

A broad, pleased grin spread across the little girl's face. "You're welcome."

She skipped away, and Grant watched her go. Instead of going back to whatever he'd been about to say before being interrupted, he smiled sadly. "You're a lucky man, Drake."

Drake was lucky at the expense of his brother spending six years in a prison camp, unbeknownst to his family, friends, and the country he served. He didn't know how to respond to that, so he didn't say anything at all.

Chapter 8

Answering the bell at five minutes after seven, Drake opened the front door to find Sheriff Graham Hughes and Officer Tad Winslow standing on the porch. "Hey, come on in. Everyone else is here."

As each man entered, he shook their hands and then led them into the living room. Shane was sitting in a wingback chair, with his husband, Tucker, standing behind him, resting his folded arms on the back of the seat. Hank and Seth had settled in on the couch, and the sheriff took the recliner while Tad sat on the empty loveseat.

"You're probably wondering why we called you all here," Lane said from where he leaned against the side of the room's fireplace.

Shane snorted. "Sounds like the beginning of a murder mystery, but now that you mention it . . ."

"Drake's got some shocking news for you first, but then we'll need your help."

Everyone's head swiveled to face Drake, who stood next to the loveseat. He took a deep breath as his stomach roiled. He never thought he'd have a conversation like this with his friends. "I . . . God, where do I start?" It was a rhetorical question. They just waited for him to explain at his own pace. "You're here because I know I can trust you all with my family's lives. I can't tell you where he's been because I don't even know the whole story, but . . . my brother, Grant, is . . . is alive, and he's here in Hazard."

"What?" The barked response was filled with shock and disbelief and had come out of everyone's mouths except for Lane and Tad, the latter not knowing the significance of the bombshell.

"What the fuck?" Shane had lowered his voice on the last word and glanced around, probably making sure none of the children had wandered into the room. They were in Trevor's room with Blair, playing Chutes and Ladders or some other board game. "Are you kidding us?"

"No, he's not." The dead-man-walking, who'd been waiting in the kitchen, entered the room through the dining area.

Shane, Seth, and Hank all jumped to their feet and gaped at Grant as if they were seeing a ghost. Well, figuratively, they were.

Paling, Hank muttered, "Holy shit." After he had a moment to recover, he added, "God, it's really you!"

The man stepped forward and embraced Grant—an emotional reunion for the two childhood friends.

"Someone want to explain what the fuck is going on?"

Tucker placed a hand on his husband's tense shoulder. "Calm down, Shane."

"Calm down? *Calm down?* What the fuck?" He quickly glanced around the room before his hard gaze landed on Grant again, his fist clenched in incredulous rage. Shane was the same age as Drake, two years younger than Grant and Hank, and they'd spent all twelve years together in school. "I watched one of my best friends grieve for his brother for years. I saw him step up to the plate and become a father to Trevor because, supposedly, *you* were dead. I watched him fall in love with Blair. And now you're back from the grave to what? Claim what's yours? Bullshit. Where the fuck have you been all this time?"

Worried his friend might throw a punch, Drake moved in front of him. "Easy, Shane. I know it's a shock, and you're pissed. That bruise on his jaw is from me, so I get where your anger is coming from. Just sit down and let him explain. Please."

Gritting his teeth, Shane glared at Grant, but after a few moments, he finally stepped back and sat again. The others also took their seats once more, with Drake sitting next to Tad. Lane and Grant remained standing.

Crossing his arms, Grant let out a heavy breath. "Eight years ago, I wasn't working for the Secret Service—I was with the CIA as an undercover agent." He held up a hand when several men opened their mouths to speak. "Let me get through this, and then I'll answer questions if possible. While I can't give you a lot of details, my death was faked, and I was thrown into a prison camp in a country that's not an ally of the US. I spent the next six years performing hard labor, being tossed into a hole in the ground, used for solitary confinement, and being beaten and tortured on a regular basis. It was basically hell on Earth, and I've got the scars to prove it." Most of them were hidden by his clothes, but he turned his left arm out and pushed up the short sleeve to show the burn marks just below his armpit—and those were the least of his scars.

In the shocked silence that ensued, he bit his bottom lip for a few moments before continuing. "Almost two years ago, word got out that I was alive, and a covert team was sent in to get me out. I spent a few weeks in a hospital in Germany before I was well enough to make it back to the States. When I found out that . . . that Drake and Blair were married with a few kids, even though Trevor is mine, I couldn't come back. It was because of a combination of reasons, and I can't expect anyone to agree with my decision to remain dead to everyone here, but it is what it is. I thought it'd be best for everyone involved if I just stayed away. I've been living in Florida. I'm no longer with the CIA—

now I'm just your average Joe working in construction."

"Then why are you here?" Although Shane's tone had softened some, he still wasn't happy about the situation.

Grant pulled his cell phone out of his back pocket and swiped the screen before tapping an icon. He handed the device to Shane, who studied it briefly before showing it to Tucker, standing behind him. As it was passed around the room, Grant continued. "That photo was texted to me yesterday from an untraceable number. Around the same time, Blair received a photo of me that was taken last week at a job site I was working at."

"Who else knows you're alive?" Graham asked. His years in law enforcement had him pushing aside any emotions to deal with the problem at hand.

"My handlers at the CIA and the team that rescued me. The hospital in Germany didn't even know my name—I was admitted under an alias. The team? I trust them—they got me settled in Florida and are helping me with this situation in any way they can. Four retired special-ops guys have been watching this house and property since last night, and one of them tailed the kids this morning when they went to their babysitters' house." Drake was startled by that bit of information. It hadn't even occurred to him then that Trevor, Regan, and Michael could've been in danger this morning. But then again, he hadn't known about the photo of Blair and Trevor until after the kids had gone to Danielle's house. "As for the Company—the CIA—too much time has passed. I don't know who I can trust there, and there's no way to know if the wrong person has found out I'm alive. I'd like to think no one there is fucking with us, but I can't be certain."

"This is where you all come in," Lane said, taking over the meeting. "We have no idea who's targeting Blair, Trevor, and Grant, nor what game they're playing. While the special-ops guys are working in shifts, watching this place, we need eyes and ears in town and the surrounding area. Whoever the unsub is, it's probably someone from Grant's past with the agency. I mean, what are the odds of someone from Hazard seeing him in Florida, recognizing him, and deciding to fuck with him?"

"Very slim," the chief responded. Like every town, they had their asshole residents, but if any of them had found out Grant was alive, they'd probably be blabbing about it to whoever would listen in order to get their fifteen minutes of local fame. The rumor mill could run rampant in Hazard Falls, and if you had information no one else had, that put you at the top of the hill until the next story broke and someone else took your place.

"Exactly. So, we're looking for someone who doesn't belong in Hazard."

"That will be hard to do with the rodeo next weekend. I've already seen a shitload of people I don't recognize in town, and it's only going to get worse," Seth said. "It'd be easier to find a needle in a haystack."

Hazard Falls hosted a huge annual Rodeo Bonanza, and each one was bigger than the last. People from all over Kansas and beyond rolled into town to attend the four-day event—some got there several days ahead of time, while others stayed a few days after it was all over. A local campground was already filling up with RVs, fifth-wheels, and tents— Liberty Campgrounds usually made forty percent of its yearly profits from the rodeo week alone. The event also increased visitors to the two bars, three restaurants, two B&Bs, and other businesses in Hazard Falls. The benefits the town reaped far outweighed the logistical nightmare the planners and police went through every year to ensure the rodeo was a fun and safe event for everyone. Between the participants, support staff, volunteers, vendors, and attendees, the Hazard Falls population would temporarily increase to over 1000 people. To help with policing, the chief coordinated with the county sheriff's department and hired off-duty members of various law enforcement agencies throughout the state. In addition to the usual patrol units, there would be officers on foot, motorcycles, ATVs, and horseback. For someone trying to blend in without raising any suspicions in Hazard Falls, the upcoming week was the one to do it in.

"Which means it'll probably come down to Grant

recognizing someone from his past," Lane replied. "But we'll still need all your eyes and ears."

"How will you explain your reincarnation to the rest of the town?" Shane asked, eying Grant. "People who knew you growing up are going to recognize you, and you can't exactly figure out who's behind this by holing up here."

"Amnesia?" he shrugged. "Honestly, I haven't thought about it, but the CIA connection must stay in this room. We can say the alleged accident at sea happened, but unbeknownst to anyone, I'd survived and made it to land with amnesia, which only recently reversed itself." It sounded farfetched, even to himself, but stranger things had happened, and no one in Hazard could refute it—except maybe the person who sent the photos.

Hank confirmed what they were probably all thinking. "Not everyone is going to believe that."

Grant held out his hands, palms up. "If you can come up with something better, I'm all ears, as long as it's not that I spent six years in a prison camp for espionage."

"Why not just say it's classified?" Tucker asked. "People assumed you worked for the Secret Service, and I'm sure there's a lot those agents can't talk about. If they ask why you didn't come back before now, tell them it's none of their damn business. It usually works for me when people get too nosy for their own good."

Shaking his head, Shane smiled for the first time

since before Grant entered the room. "That's not all you say to them, Tuck."

"True, but 'fuck off' is reserved for those who don't take the hint the first time."

Everyone chuckled, and it felt as if some of the tension had left the room. Grant eyed Lane. "I assume the police department has more than just you, the chief, and . . . Tad, is it?" He glanced at the only man in the room he hadn't met before now.

"Tad Winslow," the younger deputy said, he reached up and shook Grant's hand. "Nice to meet you, but sorry it's under these circumstances."

Lane straightened and crossed his arms. "Sorry, I forgot you two didn't know each other. Tad served on the Navy base where my Marine unit was stationed in Afghanistan. We worked with a few ghosts from the agency, so I knew having him in on this was safe. The chief and I agreed the four other officers in the department don't need to know the finer details at this point. We'll just tell them to watch for anyone who doesn't look like they belong. We'll update them on a need-to-know basis. They're good cops, but a few have some loose lips regarding family and friends."

Drake had heard Lane complain about that before. In a smaller town, where the action-packed calls for cops were few and far between, it could get boring. Boredom made some people complacent. To make up for the lack of excitement, some of the cops talked about things that they shouldn't with the public.

Grant cleared his throat, then eyed Shane, Tucker, Hank, and Seth in succession. "As Drake said, we trust you with Blair's and the children's lives. But I don't want you jeopardizing your own lives and your families. If something or someone raises your suspicions, let me or the law take care of it."

"Fuck," Shane muttered before holding out his hand. "Give me your goddamn phone."

Grant's eyebrows shot up in surprise, but he took his phone back from Drake, who'd ended up with it after the photo had been passed around. After swiping to unlock the screen, he handed the device to Shane, who quickly tapped the screen. "I'm entering all our phone numbers and sending a group text to everyone so we're all connected. As pissed as I still am at you, I think I can speak for everyone else when I say we'll do what we can to make certain Blair and the kids stay safe."

Drake would've laughed at his friend if the situation weren't so serious. While Grant didn't know it yet, Shane was Trevor's godfather. There had never been any doubt in Drake's mind that the man would step up to help in any way he could. The people of Hazard Falls protected their own, whether they hated or were mad at each other or not.

"Thank you," Grant replied. "I'm sorry I brought my past to Hazard. When it's over, I'll head back to Florida and let you get on with your lives."

Frowning, Shane stood and slapped the phone

against Grant's chest. "Stop being an ass. You don't get to just waltz back into town and then expect us to toss you into the wind again and forget all about you. Let's just catch this bastard who's pulling the strings, then you can decide whether to suck it up or throw it all away again."

That was Shane—more than once during their friendship, he'd called Drake out for being a schmuck about one thing or another. The man didn't pull any punches, although he threw a few when the situation warranted.

Ten minutes later, Lane was the last man out the door, and Blair joined Drake and Grant in the kitchen, where she busied herself cleaning the already spotless countertop. For the first time since they'd fallen in love, Drake felt uncomfortable touching or holding his wife in anyone else's presence. But he wasn't the only one feeling ill at ease.

Grant gestured toward the back door. "I meant to ask—do you have Wi-Fi in the apartment? I want to do some research and contact a few people who might be able to help narrow down who sent those photos."

"Um, yeah." Drake grabbed a Post-it notepad and pen from a junk drawer and wrote down their service ID number and password, which covered both the house and the converted barn. "There's a wireless range extender for my workshop. You should be able to access it from upstairs."

"Thanks." Grant hesitated a moment. "Uh, good night."

"Good night," Blair and Drake said quietly, in unison.

Striding out the door, Grant left them alone, and Drake studied his wife's back and hunched shoulders, wondering how to address the elephant his brother had left in his wake.

Chapter 9

Blair turned off the lamp on her nightstand, climbed into bed, and waited for Drake. Even though there were armed men watching the house, he was double-checking all the locks on the doors and windows. She'd tried to tell him she'd already done that, but, apparently, he had to see for himself that everything was locked up tight. Honestly, she didn't blame him. If she had to blame anyone, it was Grant, and she hated that fact. She was happy and relieved he was alive, but she couldn't shake the feeling that a part of Drake resented his brother's return. If he did, she understood why. He had to fear Blair would want to return to her first love. She'd only loved two men in her life—both Hadley brothers. So how did she convince Drake that, no matter who'd come into, or *back* into, their lives, she was in love with him and wouldn't give him up for anything? In an ideal world, she wouldn't have to choose between them, but the world was far from perfect. Here and now, her choice was her husband. Hell, she didn't even know Grant anymore. Maybe he had a girlfriend or even a wife in Florida. And why did that thought hurt?

Her mind flittered toward what she'd overheard Grant tell the men in the meeting earlier. She cringed at the thought of him being tortured and beaten. What had he thought about while he'd been alone in a hole in the ground? That man, Carter, had said earlier that Grant's love for her and thoughts of Blair had gotten him through years of captivity and abuse. Part of her felt like she'd failed Grant—in a different way than Carter felt. Shouldn't she have known the man she loved was still alive?

Blair thought back to the day, almost eight years ago, there'd been a knock on her and Grant's town-house just outside D.C. She'd been in the middle of making a list of all the things they needed to do to get ready for the baby they were expecting. She couldn't wait to tell Grant, but she'd been holding off so she could see his expression when he found out they were going to be parents. While it'd been a surprise, since they hadn't gotten around to getting married yet, they'd both wanted a family. When she'd answered the door, two men had identified themselves as Grant's supervisors at the Secret Service. Now, Blair wondered who they'd really been—CIA agents? Probably. She remembered collapsing onto the floor when they told her he was missing and presumed dead.

Why had she believed them? They'd never been able to produce his body, but she'd taken what they'd told her at face value. Shouldn't she have questioned them more? But she hadn't. She'd called Drake, telling him his only brother was dead and she needed him. And God bless him, Drake had been on the next flight out to D.C. he'd been able to get. He'd stood by her side as they'd held a private memorial for Grant in D.C. and another with friends a few days later in Hazard. He'd helped her pack up the entire townhouse and move it all back to Kansas. And finally, he'd cooked up the scheme to marry her, so she and her unborn child would be covered under the insurance he had through his work.

When she'd fallen for Drake, it hadn't been because he'd reminded her of Grant. Though it was obvious they were related, feature-wise, their personalities had always been completely different. Artistic Drake had been the quieter of the two, while the brainiac, Grant, had been more outgoing. Both had participated in a few non-contact sports in school, but Grant had also been on the debate team, while Drake had helped the theater club with all the backdrops and props for their plays. No, she'd fallen for Drake simply because he was him. Over the past seven years, he'd been a loving father, her best friend, and the man who'd brought her libido screaming back to life. She had to show him he was and always would be the husband she wanted.

The door to the bathroom opened, and Drake shut off the light before coming to join her in their king-sized bed. A thin sliver of moonlight peeking past the window shade let her see him. She flipped the comforter and sheet back for him.

"Thanks." He climbed in next to her, with a heavy sigh.

Once he was settled, she scooted closer, set her hand on his chest, and rested her head on his shoulder. She knew she had to take the initiative when he didn't say anything. "It's a lot to take in, isn't it?"

Seconds ticked by, and she wasn't sure if he was going to answer her. Finally, he put his hand on top of hers, holding it to his chest. "Yeah, it is. How're you doing?"

She shrugged. "Okay, I guess. I'm worried about the kids, especially Trevor. Why would anyone do this?"

"I don't know, but whoever it is, they're doing it because of Grant. It's his fault."

"We can't blame him, Drake. He couldn't have known all those years ago this would happen."

He glared down at her. "He was working for the goddamn CIA, Blair. Nothing good could've ever come out of that where you and Trevor were concerned. He fucking lied to you . . . and to me. To everyone."

Blair bit her bottom lip. She hadn't meant to make him angry again. He was right, though. If Grant had told her he'd been recruited by the CIA, she would've tried to talk him out of it. Being a Secret Service agent was one thing, but being a US spy, when your superiors might deny you worked for them if you were caught somewhere you shouldn't have been, was a completely different story.

She sat up quickly and stared at Drake. "Do you think they lied to me back then? The two men who came to tell me Grant was dead? I mean, not that they were from the Secret Service, but did they know he was still alive and left him to suffer in that prison camp, denying that the US knew anything about him?" The horrible thought spun through her mind, making her nauseous.

Putting his hand on her back, he pulled her back down, so she was cuddled against him again. His voice became soothing. "I don't know, baby. But I believe that guy, Carter. He definitely feels guilty about assuming Grant was dead, and he's lived with that for a long time. I think if he knew Grant was being held somewhere, he would've done everything he could to find him years ago."

That Blair could agree with. She'd seen the pain in Carter's eyes when he'd been telling them what he could about what'd happened. He didn't seem like the kind of man who would've given up if there had been even a *hint* that Grant was still alive.

"It's hard to accept he's here, knowing you were in love with him first," Drake whispered.

Shifting until she was straddling his hips, Blair bent down and kissed him. She let him feel the love she had for him as their tongues tangled with each other. His hands went to her waist, and he drew her nightgown up her body. Pulling back just enough for him to get the garment over her head and toss it aside, Blair squirmed as his cock hardened against her bare ass.

She cupped his jaw and lowered her mouth, pausing just a fraction away from his. "I love you, Drake. I'm *in* love with you. Nothing will ever change that."

His one arm went around her back, and the other behind her head. In one smooth move, he rolled them until he was lying on top of her. His intense gaze met hers, as he grabbed a handful of her hair. Exquisite pain shot from her scalp to her clit, making it throb. "Say it again. If needing to hear it makes me a selfish bastard, so be it, but say it again, dammit."

Blair couldn't remember Drake ever being insecure about their relationship, but, right now, he was. Lifting her pelvis, she rubbed herself against his erection. She let him see the passion and devotion she felt for him in her eyes. "I'm in love with you, Drake. Forever."

His mouth descended and took possession of hers. Their sex life was still amazing, even after all these years, but tonight, there was desperation in the way Drake made love to her. Blair offered him everything he needed and took everything he gave in return. She never wanted him to think she would leave him—not for Grant or anyone. So why was she imagining Grant was making love to her too?

LYING ON HIS TEMPORARY BED, GRANT TOSSED AND turned, trying to find a comfortable position. It wasn't the mattress's fault—it was the fact he couldn't stop thinking of Blair being by his side like she'd been years ago. He hadn't been a saint the past six months or so. He'd taken several women to bed, but always with the understanding he wouldn't be there in the morning, nor should they expect to see him again. He'd met a few of them at Donovan's and had to change where he'd been getting coffee every morning after hooking up with a curvy, blonde barista at the one he'd been stopping at. That'd kind of sucked because he still hadn't found a place that made his coffee as good as she had. Yeah, it might've been childish to not go back to where she worked, but after he'd satisfied them both that night, he had no desire to ever see her again. Why? Because she wasn't the woman he'd been desperately trying to erase from his mind for the past year—Blair.

He'd been an ass not to marry her when he'd had the chance. But they'd both been so busy, her at the French embassy and his training and then going off into the field, they'd never set a date after becoming engaged. They'd wanted to return to Hazard for their wedding, so they'd be among family and close friends, but it just never seemed to be the right time. If Grant had known how things would go down, he would've insisted on, at least, a simple courthouse ceremony, so Blair would've received survivor benefits from the government. Her and Trevor's health insurance would've been covered, and she wouldn't have needed to marry Drake.

Grant could still remember what her body had felt like under his. He only had to think of her name and he grew hard like he was now. And that had all been before he'd seen her again. Time had been extremely kind to Blair. Giving birth to three children had given her even more curves to love and revel in. She was probably about a size twelve or fourteen now, up from her former size eight, but she was even sexier now than she had been back then. What he wouldn't give to see her in all her naked glory.

Rolling onto his back, he closed his eyes and imagined what she looked like without her clothes obstructing his view. He might be breaking one of the Ten Commandments by coveting his brother's wife, but he couldn't help himself—he was probably already going to hell, so what was one more sin?

He pushed his briefs down off his hips, gripped his cock, and squeezed it hard. The tip was weeping with pre-cum, and he used it as lubrication. Was Blair's pussy still bare? He used to love it whenever she'd come home from the spa in D.C., all waxed and smooth. It'd made her ultra-sensitive, and that had turned both of them on. He doubted there was any place in Hazard where she could get that done, although she might not want to anymore after having three kids. Grant pushed the cute, little rug rats out of his mind. They didn't belong there while he was fantasizing about their mother.

In Grant's mind, Blair's heat replaced his hand as she rode him. Her tits bounced as she rocked back and forth on his shaft. He could almost reach up and tweak one of them. A groan was wrenched from his mouth as he heard her moaning, panting, and begging in his mind. His hand pumped faster, harder, and he thrust his hips up as if fucking her.

Reaching down, he cupped his balls and rolled them in his hand. It wasn't long before he felt the first signs of his impending orgasm. He lifted his chin, his head sliding down on the pillow. "Come for me, Blair. Oh, God, yes!"

With a muffled roar, Grant exploded. Multicolored lights flashed behind his eyelids as he spent himself, hot cum shooting onto his abdomen. He gasped for air as he came down from the sensual high of the endorphins coursing through his body.

He imagined Blair collapsing on top of him in post-coital bliss. Kissing his cheek, she whispered, "That was wonderful. I love you . . . Drake."

Grant's eyes flew open. *Dammit!*

Chapter 10

"Hey, Blair," Betty Lou called from the other end of the grocery store aisle. "You must be psychic. I was going to call you in just a few minutes."

Blair smiled at her friend who owned the Bar None, having taken it over after her father's heart attack. That was the one thing about small towns—it was rare to not run into someone you knew who wanted to chat. At least Lou was someone Blair didn't mind seeing at the moment. She'd asked Drake to watch the kids for a bit after breakfast, needing some space from him and Grant, both of whom had been broody this morning. The awkwardness that filled the air anytime Grant was in the room was starting to drive her nuts, but she didn't want him to leave. If he did, she was afraid he'd disappear forever.

The two women met in the middle of the aisle, and

Lou lowered her voice, almost to a whisper, to avoid being heard by anyone on either side of the fully stocked shelves. "How're you doing? Lane stopped by the bar last night and told me about Grant. I still can't believe it."

Blair had known the men had discussed sharing the information with Lou since her bar/restaurant was popular with locals and visitors alike. If anyone was in a position to meet any strangers in town, it was Lou or the owners of the Moody Moon Motel. The place was far from being a Hilton, but from what she'd been told, the rooms were always clean—not that she'd ever been in any of them. It was one of those places in Hazard she drove by a few times every week but had never needed to stop at. There were also two B&Bs in town, but, apparently, Lane was going to be quietly investigating their current guests.

She was a little surprised Lou had said Lane's name without the usual annoyance in her tone. Blair had no idea what'd happened between the two, who'd been a couple in high school, but while Lane seemed determined to win Lou back one of these days, she was fighting it tooth and nail. Maybe she was finally softening to him. But that was another story.

"Neither can I." Blair shook her head. "I mean, it honestly feels like a *Lifetime* movie, you know? I still catch my breath when he walks into the room. It's like seeing a ghost but knowing he's real."

"I can only imagine. How's Drake taking it?"

"Hard. I can tell his shock, relief, and anger are still battling each other in his mind. I mean, we both kind of understand why Grant didn't let us know he was alive, after finding out Drake and I had gotten married and had more kids, but it doesn't make it any easier to accept."

Lou's eyes widened. "Does he know Trevor is his?"

Pretty much everyone in Hazard knew her oldest son was Grant's and that she and Drake had originally married for the insurance, but they'd also accepted the couple had fallen in love over time and were happy for them. The gossip over their marriage of convenience had died down years ago. "Yeah, he does, but he's agreed Trevor is too young to understand it yet. Maybe in a few years . . ." She shrugged. "For now, the kids are all calling him Uncle Grant. I'm just really worried about who sent Grant and me those photos."

"Lane mentioned those but didn't give me all the details. He just said to stay quiet about it and to keep an eye out for anyone who seems out of place."

"I wish I could tell you more than you probably already know, but, honestly, I don't know much more than that either. What I do know is that whatever happened back then, Grant said it's classified." Well, technically, that was what she was supposed to say if anyone asked her.

Lou crossed her arms and harrumphed. "I guess that's why they call it the *Secret* Service. Is he really going to keep the rest of Hazard in the dark about him being alive? I mean, someone is going to recognize him sooner or later, and the gossip mill will be buzzing for weeks when that happens."

"I don't know, but, for now, we're supposed to keep it between ourselves. Shane, Tucker, and Hank got permission to tell Paige and Nicole since the two of them can sniff out any lie or half-truth their husbands tell them, but they're also being sworn to secrecy. Someone wanted Grant to return to Hazard— we just don't know who or why yet."

"Well, I'll keep my eyes open for trouble and my mouth shut if anyone asks why. But if you need to talk, call me."

Blair gave her a grateful smile. "Thanks."

"Shit, here comes Bridget."

Glancing over her shoulder, Blair saw the Hazard Falls' combination snob, bitch, and tramp, with her teased hair, painted eyes, lips, and nails, and silicone-enhanced face and tits, and she was walking in their direction. Bridget Kline was the town's longtime mayor's daughter, and she took that to mean the local residents were her royal subjects, despite being put in her place several times by those who'd had enough of her superior attitude. The woman sneered as she approached. "Well, look who we have here. Who let you out of your bat cave so early in the day, Betty Lou?"

Never one to rise to Bridget's bait, Lou smiled sweetly. "Probably the same person who let a certain bleached-blonde bimbo out of hers. Now that the pleasantries are out of the way, what do you want, Bridget?"

Not responding, the woman eyed Lou in distaste for a moment before turning to Blair. "I'd like you to talk to your husband, Blair. I want him to make some new bookcases for my office, but he said he can't do it before the new year. That's not exactly the way to run a business, you know. Time is money."

"Well, I'm sorry about that . . ." No, she wasn't. "But Drake has been very busy. I know he's not guaranteeing new orders for six months, at the very least." That much was true. His reputation had grown tremendously over the past few years, and he'd been able to leave his construction job and still ensure their bills were paid, including their health insurance. There was even some money left over at the end of each month to add to Blair's income, which went toward their savings. During next January's winter break, they were planning to surprise the kids with the trip to Disney World Trevor had been dreaming of.

"If he said he can't do it, then there's nothing I can do to help you." Not that she would anyway.

Bridget turned up her nose. "Well, then, I'll just have to take my business elsewhere. There are plenty of carpenters out there, who are more talented than him."

Without saying goodbye to either woman, Bridget spun around and sashayed down the aisle in her five-inch stiletto heels. How she didn't break her neck in those things was always a mystery to Blair. Leaning toward Lou, she lowered her voice. "What office is she talking about? Since when does Bridget work at all?"

"Oh, you didn't hear yet? Daddy Dearest gave her the money to open an art gallery up the street in Rusty Carlson's place." The elderly man had run a second-hand store out of the bottom half of his Main Street home, much to the embarrassment of the mayor's office. Richard Kline had been trying to get the business shut down for years, but Rusty's house had been grandfathered in for both a residential and commercial occupancy long ago. When Rusty passed away last year, leaving behind no will or known relatives, the town had seized the property under the guise of an unpaid tax lien. The merchandise and personal belongings that'd filled both levels of the house and the front and side yards had been sold off, cheap, to a thrift store owner from the next town over. The old man's meager savings in the bank had been just enough to pay for a proper funeral and burial in the local cemetery, which had been attended by most of the town. Rusty had been the type of man who'd always given someone a break if they needed it, and who'd usually been the first person to volunteer to help out a neighbor. Blair wasn't the only townsperson who missed him.

"What the hell does Bridget know about art? And who does she think is going to buy it?" Most people Blair knew had maybe one or two paintings in their homes with the rest of the wall space decorated with family photos or western-themed displays. They certainly wouldn't be spending money on high-priced art and that was most likely what Bridget would be trying to sell.

"Who the hell knows? Apparently, they think an art gallery would be good for tourism. She's opening it next month but already has contracted some artists from the county and Garden City to showcase a few pieces during the rodeo." Dozens of vendors rented out tent space each year, and there was always a wide variety of merchandise to browse through and food to enjoy when one wasn't watching the events.

"I'm surprised she didn't approach Drake for a piece —although, she may have, and he just blew her off. *That* wouldn't surprise me.

Lou pulled her cell phone out of her back pocket and glanced at the screen for the time. "Listen, I have to get going. I've got a liquor delivery coming to the bar in a little bit. But if you need me for anything, call, and I'll also let the guys know if I see anyone suspicious."

After giving Lou a quick hug goodbye, Blair tried to refocus her attention on her shopping list. But her brief respite from thinking about Grant was over now that she was alone in her thoughts again. If only she could dismiss him from her mind and return to the pleasant life she'd been experiencing just a few days ago. Unfortunately, that wasn't going to happen any time soon. Now that she was over her initial shock at him being alive, she didn't know how she felt about him returning to Florida after everything was over.

Chapter 11

Muttering a curse in irritation, Grant disconnected the call to one of the men, a retired SEAL, keeping an eye on the place. The guy had nothing new to report. Grant was starting to feel bad for them. They'd been rotating shifts over the past two days, with one working 6:00 am to 2:00 pm, another taking over until 10:00 pm, while the other two teamed up for the overnight. Unfortunately, or fortunately, depending on how one looked at it, they hadn't seen anyone suspicious near the property. They'd also been keeping their ears to the ground in town when they weren't crashing at the RV one of them owned. It was parked at the Liberty Campgrounds since there'd been no occupancy at the Moody Moon or the B&Bs in town due to the rodeo.

There also hadn't been any news from Brody when Grant had spoken to him a little while ago. Whoever had sent the photos to Grant and Blair hadn't used a throwaway phone, as they'd expected. Instead, they'd been sent from a dummy email account that had gone through dozens of IP addresses worldwide. Brody still hadn't been able to trace it to the original account. Whoever had sent it was as good a hacker as the Trident geeks were, and the bastard was taking his fucking time in letting Grant know what his next move was.

In the meantime, Grant was going nuts being this close to the woman he still loved, deep down in his heart, knowing she'd never be his again. Every interaction she had with Drake and the children he'd observed just reminded Grant of what could've been his if things had gone differently. The unfairness of it all churned in his gut, combined with anger, jealousy, and regret.

Sticking his phone into the back pocket of his jeans, Grant strode across the yard to the back porch of the house. Drake was in his workshop, and hopefully, Blair was busy with the children or some housework. Grant would fill up a travel mug with coffee, then start driving around town again, looking for anyone familiar or out-of-place. He needed the caffeine since he'd slept like shit last night. He'd awakened twice, thanks to his nightmares, reliving what he'd gone through in North Korea. After the second time, he hadn't gone back to sleep. Instead, he'd gotten on the computer and began reading some of his old files from his time with the Company. He was hoping something or someone would stand out to him, but nothing had as of yet.

When he entered the kitchen, Blair simultaneously came in from the hallway, carrying a load of dirty clothes to the attached laundry room. "Oh! Um . . . I mean, sorry, I . . . um . . . didn't know you were in here."

He tore his gaze from her, trying not to show her how she affected him. His heart rate increased, his cock twitched in his jeans, and his mouth salivated. His brain acted like he had x-ray vision, and her clothes seemed to fall away before his very eyes. Shaking the image from his mind, he stepped toward the Keurig machine on the counter and hit the button to heat the water. "Just came in for some coffee before I head out."

She dropped the laundry basket in the other room before returning. "If you . . . um . . . have clothes you want me to throw into the washing machine, just bring them over."

"I don't need you to play house for me, Blair."

"Excuse me?" Her annoyed tone had him turning to face her. She glared at him as she crossed her arms. "*Play house?* What the hell does that mean, Grant? I don't 'play' house. I work hard, raising three children, cleaning, doing laundry, cooking, and everything else that comes with having a family and home. And on top of all that, I have my translation business."

He couldn't help himself. The frustration and anxiety from the last few days were taking their toll. Pointing a finger at her, Grant sneered. "Is that all?

Because I would've killed for all of that for the six years I was in that hellhole, so don't expect any sympathy from me. I never knew when my next meal was coming. I never knew if I'd see the next sunrise. Clean clothes? Yeah, forget those. No . . . no, you get no sympathy from me, Blair. While I didn't know if the ditch I was digging was going to be a latrine or my grave, you were here in Hazard, sleeping in a nice comfy bed with my fucking brother and—"

His rant was cut off by her hand slapping his cheek, narrowly missing his jaw, which was still sore from Drake's punch. The *crack* sounded like a bomb going off in the room. Grant was more stunned than hurt, although the strike had stung.

While it was evident Blair was just as shocked as he was, there was still ire flaring in her eyes. She lowered her voice, probably so the kids wouldn't hear her over whatever TV show they were watching in the family room. "Don't you dare dump that all on me. I'm sorry for what you went through, Grant. I wouldn't wish that on my worst enemy, let alone someone I loved. But none of that was my fault. I thought you were dead. You left me alone and pregnant and wondering how I would take care of our unborn child. I didn't qualify for survivor benefits since we weren't married, and I could barely function those first few months.

"Damn you!" Tears rolled down her red cheeks, but she didn't wipe them away. "What was I supposed to do? Dig my own grave and crawl into it? Trust me, there were times during my pregnancy when the little life inside of me—the only living thing I had left of you—was the only reason I didn't give in to my grief. Drake didn't have to do what he did. I sure as hell never expected him to suggest we should get married, but he did. And whether you want to hear it or not, he was the second-best thing to happen to me since I found out you were allegedly dead—the first thing is my children. That first year, Drake became my lifeline—he and Trevor. Drake forced me to get out of bed every morning instead of letting me lie there with the lights out and shades down, being miserable. Did you expect me to be the grieving widow for the next forty or fifty years of my life? Instead of being jealous or angry or whatever you're feeling about your brother, you should be fucking grateful he was there for me—he was there when *you* weren't. So, don't you dare accuse me of having things easy while you were suffering. I wasn't beaten and tortured physically, like you, but let me tell you, I was tortured mentally and emotionally—in a different way than you were, but I suffered. And then one day . . . one beautiful day, I gave birth to your son, and I finally realized I had something worth living for again. I had a future—not with you, but with your legacy . . . and with Drake. So, don't dump all that on me, Grant Hadley, because I won't stand for it."

Pivoting, she stormed out of the kitchen and down the hallway, never giving him a moment to get a word in. Hell, he wasn't sure if she'd taken a single breath during her rant. Damn, he was an ass. Why couldn't he stop putting his fucking foot in his mouth? He didn't want to hurt her, but that's all he seemed to be doing since his arrival.

He had to get out of there. Not out of Hazard because there was still the question of a threat against Blair and Trevor, but he had to get out of the house for a while.

Ignoring the coffee maker, Grant left the kitchen the same way he'd come in and headed for his SUV. After climbing into the driver's seat, he shut the door and started the engine. But before putting the gear in drive, he stared out the window at where he'd grown up. While the original structures, trees, and land-scaping were the same, there had been many updates made. It was more than just a house—it was a home again. Something it hadn't felt like since his mother had died. But it wasn't his anymore. It was Drake and Blair's home, and it was filled with love and laughter—at least, it had been until he'd shown up.

"You did what?" Paige Wilson asked as she gaped at her friend.

Sitting at Paige's kitchen table, Blair let out a heavy sigh, her eyes swollen and red from the tears that'd finally stopped running down her cheeks. She was still mortified about what she'd done twenty minutes ago, but she needed to talk to the only woman she knew who might understand what she was going through. "I slapped Grant across the face. I've never done that to anyone in my life, but he just pissed me off, and it happened before I realized what I was doing."

"So, he deserved it."

Blair dipped her chin and glared at Paige. "Yes, he was being an ass, but no, he didn't deserve that—not after all he's gone through." She almost slipped and mentioned he'd been in a prison camp, but she'd promised Grant she wouldn't repeat that to anyone.

"After all *he's* gone through? What about you and Drake? Grant just waltzes back to Hazard after, what—seven or eight years of you thinking he was dead—and everyone is treating him with kid gloves. You went through just as much crap as he did, in my opinion, so he gets no sympathy from me about you smacking him."

Blair smiled for the first time since she'd arrived at the Red River Ranch—Paige was a good friend. She hadn't lived in Hazard until about two years ago and didn't know Grant other than the stories she'd heard about him, but she had no trouble defending Blair against him.

"Can I ask you a question, but it has to stay between us?" Blair asked.

"Of course. Tuck's not the only one in this family

who can tell others it's none of their damn business. What's up?"

She hesitated momentarily, then blurted out, "How do you do it? I mean, how do you love two men at the same time and not have any jealousy or anything between all of you?"

A grin spread across Paige's face. "I was wondering if you were going to ask me that. You're in love with Drake, yet all those feelings for Grant are still there, too, aren't they?"

Nodding her head, she replied, "Yes, and it's so damn confusing. I love Drake, and it's not out of gratitude for helping me all those years ago. I can't see my life without him. But Grant . . . I never stopped loving him, even though I thought he was dead. Before he came back to Hazard, I still had fantasies about him—about making love to him again—but I could never tell Drake that. It would hurt him. And now that Grant is a reality again and not just a fantasy, I-I don't know what to do. I love them both, Paige, and it's a nightmare."

Leaning forward, Paige placed her hand on Blair's. "Let me answer your question. How do I love Tuck and Shane at the same time, with no jealousy on anyone's part? I just do. They are so different, yet I can't imagine one without the other. To me, they're two halves of a whole." She leered and raised her eyebrows several times in quick succession. "And watching them have sex is hotter than Hades, not that it's something Grant and Drake would do, I'm sure."

"Yeah, as brothers, that's completely off the table. But in the ménages we read in the book club, there are a bunch of brothers who love one woman, and they make it work. If I didn't know you, Shane, and Tucker, I would think all those books were complete fiction, but ménages do exist, and your marriage is living proof."

"Are you saying you think Grant and Drake might be interested in a ménage relationship?"

She shook her head. "I don't know. And I don't know if I'm interested in one, but I can't imagine Grant leaving at some point and just being the uncle my kids know down in Florida, who they only see once every three years or so. I know he's still attracted to me—I can feel his eyes on me all the time, and it's so difficult not to respond to him. I know it's only been a week, but my heart is breaking in two just thinking about not seeing him every day. I don't even know how to approach Grant and Drake about it. What if Drake thinks I'm only interested in Grant, and I'm asking to try a ménage in order to have my cake and eat it too?"

"Then we'll have to figure out a way to let them both know that you're not throwing either one of them to the curb." Paige bit her bottom lip. "And I think I have an idea that just might work."

Before Blair could ask for details, Paige's step-daughter, nine-year-old Arianna, yelled from down the hallway. "Mom! Ashley's awake!"

Paige got to her feet. "Don't go anywhere. Let me

just change her diaper, and we'll talk more while I feed her."

As her friend hurried down the hallway to get her one-year-old daughter, Blair's mind spun. Was she really thinking about a ménage relationship with Grant and Drake? Would they be willing to try it, or would it destroy her marriage? If that happened, she'd never forgive herself.

Chapter 12

Staring at but not paying attention to the ESPN commentators on the wide-screen TV over the dozens of assorted liquor bottles, Grant took another sip of whiskey. He welcomed the smooth burn as it traveled past his throat to his stomach. It was just after 3:00 p.m. at Bar None, and there were only a few sad sacks like him sitting at the bar between lunch and dinner. Aside from the male bartender asking what he wanted to drink when Grant had first sat down, no one had tried to engage him in conversation, which was fine with him. With his beard and mustache growing out and the dimness of the room, none of the old timers at the other end of the bar had recognized him, although he remembered them from years ago. Surprisingly, they hadn't changed much. Grant envied them because he'd changed more in almost eight years than most people did in their entire lives. Confinement and torture would do that to a man.

After driving around aimlessly for two hours, his vehicle seemed to steer its way to the bar. His cheek and conscience still smarted from Blair's slap and his own stupid mouth, which didn't seem to want to cooperate with his mind. His heart, brain, and body were at war with each other whenever he was in the same room with Blair. It wasn't his intention to hurt her, but the longer he stayed with her and Drake, the more he wanted her, which made him an asshole. He just wished whoever had orchestrated their unexpected reunion would show his or her cards and let Grant take care of them before returning to Florida. He wouldn't be constantly reminded there that he was still in love with Blair but couldn't have her. If he tried to claim what used to be his, he'd destroy the happy life she and Drake had made for themselves and the children.

The barstool next to him scraped the floor when it was moved, and someone sidled in next to him, taking the seat. Tucker Wilson must have come through the bar's rear entrance. Dressed in a gray T-shirt, faded Wranglers, worn black shit-kickers, and a straw cowboy hat, he flagged down the bartender, threw some money on the bar, and pointed to Grant's near-empty glass. "Give him another, Dean, and I'll take whatever he's having too."

With a nod, the man retrieved a bottle of Jack Daniels, poured the Tennessee whiskey into two new tumblers since Grant was still holding his, and then set both on the bar. "What's the special occasion, Tuck? You're never here this early unless you're having lunch with the family."

He shrugged. "Nothing, really. Just came into town to run a few errands and decided to stop for a drink."

Dean seemed to accept that answer before striding down to the opposite end of the bar to wait on another customer who'd walked in behind Tucker. Grant picked up his new drink and huffed. "Thought you were the one who told people what you do isn't any of their fucking business."

"Only after they don't take the first hint. After that, all bets are off. That is, as long as I don't have my girls with me. I try to curb my annoyance when Paige, Arianna, and Ashley are around." He took a sip of his whiskey. "But when it comes to friends, butting in is just another way to say we care about each other."

Grant glared at him. "Since when did we become friends?" Tucker had only moved to Hazard and started working at the Triple-R about three years before Grant's alleged death. Grant and Blair had met him several times when they'd returned to Kansas for a few visits, but that was ages ago. The man was now married to Shane, and they were both married to Paige, their second wife, after they had been widowed a few years earlier. Grant had no idea how that all worked—they had to have a huge fucking bed—and he didn't really care. To each their own.

"We're not." Tucker's gaze remained on ESPN. "But I'm friends with Drake and Blair, so that makes you a friend-in-law, I guess."

"Is there such a thing?"

"Who the hell knows?" A few moments of silence passed between them before Tucker asked, "So when this is all over, are you leaving your heart in Hazard and tucking your tail between your legs while you head back to Florida, or what?"

Grant's glass-filled hand froze on its way to his mouth, and he gaped at the man beside him. "What the fuck are you talking about?"

Turning on his stool, Tucker faced him. "What I mean is, you're in love with Blair, Drake's in love with Blair, and she's in love with both of you. So, why don't you and Drake share Blair?" If nothing else, the man was blunt.

"Are you nuts?"

"Nope. And trust me when I say that before our first wife, Sarah, came into Shane's and my lives, a ménage marriage used to be as foreign to me as it is to you."

Grant downed half his new glass of whiskey. For this conversation, he needed it. "You do realize I have no desire to have an incestuous relationship with my own brother, right?"

"Oh, for fuck's sake," Tucker muttered while rolling his eyes. "Why would you even think that's what I was implying? I'm not telling you to have sex with your brother—God, that's sick. Not everyone needs to be doing everyone to have a three-way relationship. There are a lot of guys out there who're involved in ménages, where they're both heterosexual, and some of them are brothers. Look at Remi and Grayson Mann, the record producers. They're twin brothers and engaged to one woman. And the only reason I know that is Paige was watching one of those reality wedding shows the other day, and their fiancée was on it, picking out a dress to wear."

"Actually, I know them. They live in Clearwater Beach near Tampa." Now that they were mentioned, Grant remembered the trio he'd met once or twice at Shelby and Parker's barbecues. The Mann brothers' business, Black Diamond Records, was one of the world's top recording production companies. At first, Grant had thought it was weird they were in a ménage relationship, but they were members of Ian and Devon Sawyer's BDSM club, and apparently, *weird* was normal there. In fact, Grant recalled another threesome that the Sawyer brothers' cousin was involved in, although he couldn't remember the guy's name—Matt or Mitch or something like that. His relationship was similar to the one Tucker was in—all three were in love with each other.

"Seriously?"

"Yeah, they're friends with my boss and a few other people I know. But I only met them a couple of times at parties."

Tucker finally took another sip from his glass. "Well, there you go."

When the other man didn't elaborate, Grant gaped at him. "There I go, where? What the hell are you talking about? Drake and Blair would never go for a ménage—with me or anyone else." Would they? And was he honestly thinking about it? "I mean, maybe it works for you and other people, but it's not for us. Besides, I'm not the man either of them used to know —a lot has changed. Blair deserves better than a man who still has nightmares every night—she's better off with Drake."

That was the first time he'd ever admitted to having nightmares to anyone other than his shrink. He had no idea why he'd confessed to it now, but he hadn't said anything that wasn't true. It was one of the reasons why he'd never stayed the whole night with any of the women he'd taken to bed in Tampa. He didn't want anyone to see him wake in a terrified panic, thinking he was back in that hellhole.

Sighing, his drinking partner waved the bartender over again. "Fill him back up, Dean, and put an order of hot wings into the kitchen for me. I'm fucking hungry, and this conversation will take a while."

CLIMBING OUT OF HIS TRUCK, SHANE CLOSED THE DOOR and strode toward Drake's workshop. He'd been doing the week's payroll when his wife had walked into his office with Ashley in her arms. Shane had briefly said hello to Drake's wife when she'd first arrived with the kids, but he'd left Blair and Paige to have some tea and girl talk while he tried to get some work done. However, when Paige had come to him with her little scheme to unite Grant, Blair, and Drake into one big happy ménage, Shane had been all too willing to help. To him, it was an obvious solution to their problem, but he doubted his good friend would be easy to convince the plan could work.

Shane pushed the door open and entered the workshop. The whir of Drake's jigsaw kept Shane from calling out to his friend. There was no need to startle the man and risk him losing a finger or two. After giving Roscoe, who'd been lying near the door, an ear scratch, Shane moved cautiously into Drake's line of vision and waited, inspecting several completed and in-progress pieces of furniture and sculptures. It still amazed Shane how Drake could take a fallen tree and make it into a work of art. When they'd been much younger, Drake had learned to whittle pieces of wood from his grandfather. Even back then, the guy had shown some amazing talent. Shane still had several small, carved figurines in his office that Drake had given him while still in high school.

When the saw shut off, Shane turned back to his friend. "Keeping busy, I see."

"I'm *always* busy these days. I've got orders that'll take me well into the new year. What're doing here in the middle of the day?"

"Your wife and kids are at my house with my wife and kids and one of the special-ops tails. Talk about mayhem and bedlam. I couldn't concentrate on the payroll anymore, so I decided to go for a ride. The truck kind of just steered its way over here."

Yeah, that was a lie, but he wasn't about to tell Drake he was there because Paige had instructed him to talk Drake into trying a ménage relationship with Blair and Grant. It was Tucker's job to have the same chat with Grant. Shane had no idea why more people weren't in ménages. It was so comforting to know that Paige and Tucker would be there for each other if something happened to him. He wouldn't be leaving either one of them alone. When his first wife, Sarah, passed away after a brave fight against cancer, Shane dealt with it far better than his husband had. But helping Tuck and their then four-year-old daughter, Ari, through their grief and depression had helped prevent Shane from falling into the same dismal abyss. Together, they'd healed each other, and when Paige had walked into their lives two years later, she'd brought with her a bright future for all of them.

Shane ran his hand over a finished dining table that could seat about twelve people. "Nice work, as always."

Leaning his ass against a tool bench, Drake crossed his arms as his eyes narrowed. "You didn't come here to talk about furniture, Shane. So, what do you want to talk about?"

Shrugging, Shane sat on a nearby stool. "I don't know. Maybe your combined anger, hurt, jealousy, relief, fear, and all the other emotions churning through your gut since Grant's reincarnation."

Drake pivoted and gave Shane his back, mindlessly picking up tools and setting them back down. "I don't know what you're talking about."

"Oh, don't give me that bullshit, man. I know you better than almost anyone else around and vice versa. Hell, you were the first person I told when I figured out I liked both guys and girls back in high school. I still remember your response—'So? What's that got to do with what you want on the damn pizza?'"

It was true. Shane blurted out he was bisexual while Drake had been getting ready to call in a delivery order when they'd been hanging out in the house across the driveway one night while Drake's dad had been out somewhere. Drake's response had shocked Shane more than his own realization about his sexual attraction to both men and women.

After setting his hands flat atop the tool bench, Drake dropped his head down. "I'm scared shitless, Shane. I'm so afraid Blair will choose Grant over me that I wish he were still dead to us. And that makes me a heartless bastard, doesn't it? Some fucking brother I am. I can't even be happy he's alive and well because he's put my family and marriage in danger. I almost hate him for what he did to us. What he's still doing to us."

Sighing, Shane stood and strode over to his friend. "I get it, Drake. I do. I still have to keep my anger in check when I think about it all. But I'll get over it someday, and so will you."

"He still loves her. And despite her love for me, I know she still loves him too."

"So, build on that."

Standing erect again, Drake glared at Shane. "What are you talking about?"

"Share Blair—God, I'll have that rhyme in my head all day now. Just kidding—about the rhyme, not the sharing part." Shane snorted. "Stop looking at me like I have three heads. Look, you have no problem with my threesome. It's weird to some people, but you've always accepted it without prejudice. So, instead of worrying about which one of you Blair will choose, why give her a choice? You're both in love with her. She's in love with both of you. Instead of looking at how things could go to shit, look at how you and Grant can care for your woman together." He gestured toward all the different projects Drake was in the middle of. "You just said you're busy as hell lately. I know Blair has to do her work at night because you're splitting the child-rearing and household chores, and that's when you take over for her. You're both exhausted by the time the day is done, right? Well, add Grant into the mix. He can help take care of all that and give you both the breathing room I know you've been missing lately. Raising three kids is tough, I know that, and I only have two." He grinned. "But that'll change in about seven months."

Drake's eyes widened. "Paige is pregnant again?"

"Hell, yeah. Not sure if it was my super sperm or Tucker's this time, but yeah, she told us the other day. It's safe to let the cat out of the bag now because she also told Nicole yesterday and Blair today." Shaking his head, he continued. "But getting back to you, Blair, and Grant. Instead of worrying about losing her, why not bring Grant into your relationship? I know two brothers who share their wife—well, I don't know them personally, but they're friends with my cousin, Quinn. The sexual logistics aren't as bad as you might think they are—you just have to get over any embarrassment of your junk accidentally brushing up against his junk. It happens, no matter how hard you try not to let it. Of course, I don't have that problem with Tuck."

"T.M.I., my friend." Drake let out a heavy sigh. "I don't know about this. Hell, *if*—and that's a big *if*—if I decide to go through with this, what if it's not what Blair wants or what Grant even wants? What if we try it, and everything goes to hell?"

"And what if you try it and everything goes right? As for Blair, I'm sure the idea has crossed her mind at least once since Grant's come home."

"What? She said something to you today?"

"Me? No, we just said hello to each other." That was true. He hadn't discussed his pending visit with Drake with her because she'd been putting lunch together for the kids who'd joined her in the kitchen while Shane had been talking with Paige. "If she confided in anyone, it would be my wife. But since Blair reads ménage romance, I'm sure—"

"What?" The question was practically shouted in disbelief. If Drake's eyebrows were any higher, they'd be in his hair. "What are you talking about?"

Shane snorted in amusement. "You're kidding me, right? You don't know what books your wife reads and translates? She's in that book club with Paige, Nicole, and a bunch of other women—trust me when I say they love reading ménage romance. And I know they've gotten some of their books because of Blair's recommendations after she's translated them. Dude, get ahold of her e-reader one of these days. Some of those books are fucking hot. Tuck and I have Paige read us the sex scenes some nights, and I don't think she's ever gotten more than halfway through before we attack her."

"Seriously?"

"Yes, seriously. Try it sometime." He glanced at his watch. "Anyway, I've got to get back home, but promise me you'll think about the ménage. I honestly think it will be the best thing for all three of you."

Twenty minutes later, Shane and Paige assured

Blair they had no problem with her kids sleeping over any night she needed if the scheme came to fruition. Shane would make sure the special-ops guys knew what was happening and set up a schedule with his ranch hands to help keep an eye on things while Trevor, Regan, and Michael were there. He just hoped Blair, Drake, and Grant would take the opportunity to open their minds and hearts and make it work between them.

Chapter 13

Two days later . . .

As the other men gathered in the large workshop, Drake leaned against his tool bench. It'd been six days since Grant had been resurrected from the dead—at least, that's how Drake kept thinking about it—and they were still no closer to figuring out who'd sent the photos to Grant and Blair. Instead of being relieved nothing had happened, everyone seemed antsier and more frustrated. And Drake was worrying even more about losing his wife, although she'd been trying to reassure him all week she wasn't going to leave him. However, he hadn't missed the way Grant watched Blair with a combination of regret and lust in his eyes, nor had he missed the sadness on Blair's face whenever she looked at Grant. The only thing Drake could hope for was that they figured out what the hell was going on, so his brother no longer had an excuse to stay in Hazard. And, once more, Drake felt like a bastard for wanting Grant to disappear again so his marriage would be safe.

Drake also couldn't stop thinking about his conversation with Shane the other day. Was a ménage really something the three of them could do? Was Drake willing to share his wife with his brother? They'd be subject to the same ridicule the Wilsons were from the small-minded people in town. Did Drake want to subject his wife and kids to that? And speaking of the kids, would it be fair to both Trevor and Grant to have the boy think his biological father was his uncle, at least until he was old enough to understand? When the time came for *that* awkward conversation, would Trevor hate them for not telling him sooner? God, there was so much on Drake's mind, it was a miracle he could get through the day without going insane.

Looking around his workshop, Drake was once again reminded that his family was in danger—the question was, from whom? Lane, Tad, Graham, Shane, Tucker, and Seth had all arrived within the last few minutes while Grant was pacing back and forth as he spoke on his phone with someone named Brody down in Florida. Meanwhile, Victor Price, one of the former Navy SEALs watching over Blair and the kids, was on his cell phone with Ian Sawyer. Since things were getting drawn out, Vic was arranging for a few more special-ops guys to come in and give the others a break and expand the rotation schedule. Drake had been surprised to learn that Carter had insisted on paying for the extra security as long as they were needed. It had to cost the guy a pretty penny, but if that's what it took to ease his guilt-ridden mind, then Drake was all for it. While he and Blair were making decent money in their respective careers and had saved quite a bit, he doubted he could afford to pay eight highly trained men to guard his family. The same went for Grant—working in construction could pay well, but not *that* well.

While his friends were trying to learn who was behind this whole mess and what their end game was, Grant had been cruising around town during the day and night, looking for anyone familiar from his past with the agency. So far, with his facial hair growing out, a pair of dark sunglasses or fake reading ones, and a baseball cap, he'd managed to avoid being recognized by the residents of Hazard, but that'd probably been just sheer luck. No one would expect to see a ghost from over eight years ago—the last time Grant had visited Hazard with Blair. It also helped that the number of people walking around town had increased exponentially for the rodeo, which started in three days.

Price disconnected his call and then turned to greet everyone. Within thirty seconds, Drake's brother did the same. The frustration on Grant's face was palpable, and Drake's stomach sank. Obviously, he hadn't received good news.

Thrusting his hands into his hair, Grant said, "Brody and Nathan have been hammering the Dark Web, trying to knock some prevalent intel out of it, but so far, they've got nothing."

Crossing his arms, Price leaned against the tool bench next to Drake. "If those two can't find it, I doubt it exists. Sawyer pays those guys a lot of money because they're both very good at what they do."

"So, if they can't find anything, there's likely no hit on my head or Trevor's or Blair's heads either."

"Which means what?" Seth asked, voicing the same question running through Drake's mind.

"It's personal," Price answered. "So, now the question is, who did you piss off, Hadley?"

Throwing his hands in the air, Grant shook his head. "How the fuck do I know? If it's someone from my private life before I was captured, there's a billion to one chance they suddenly spotted me in Florida and recognized me. No one in my current life down there can connect me to Hazard except Carter, Sawyer, and the Trident team, and I trust them. So, that leaves my professional life—someone at the agency or someone who knew I was with the agency, who recently found out I'm not dead and holds a grudge for some reason."

"Or someone who was behind the espionage charges and outed you in the first place."

Grant froze in place and stared at the retired SEAL. "A traitor?"

Price shrugged. "It's been known to happen—Sawyer agrees it's possible. Whoever this asshole is, he's biding his time and drawing out the anticipation."

"So, he's not just going to go away?" No one answered Drake's rhetorical question. As the days ticked by, he'd hoped that whoever sent the photos hadn't done it for nefarious reasons and they just wanted Grant to return to his family.

A thought crossed Drake's mind, and as it took hold, it brought his anger raging to the surface again. He glared at his older brother. Why hadn't he thought of this before? "Or does this asshole not exist at all?"

His eyes narrowing, Grant stared at him in confusion. "What are you talking about?"

He wasn't the only one in the room with a bewildered look on his face.

Pushing off the bench, Drake took two threatening steps forward and dodged Shane's hand when he tried to stop him. "What I mean, *brother*, is did you make up this phantom photographer and send those pictures yourself so you'd have an excuse to come back to Hazard, play the hero, and win the girl again?"

Everyone else in the workshop went perfectly still as the question hung heavily in the air between the two brothers.

Grant gaped at Drake as if he'd grown horns and then sneered. "When did you become such an asshole?"

Without conscious thought, Drake lunged for him, but Tucker and Shane were faster and stopped his forward momentum with their muscular bodies. Lane and the chief appeared ready to grab Grant, but he clearly wasn't willing to dive into a fight with Drake. Instead, he shook his head in disgust. "You have no idea why I didn't come back to Hazard during the past year and a half, do you? You still haven't figured it out." He used his thumb to poke himself in the sternum. "I couldn't. Once I heard you and Blair were married with kids . . . with *my* kid calling you 'Dad' . . . I couldn't come back. I couldn't put Blair in a position where she felt she had to choose between us. I couldn't face her choosing you over me. And . . . and I couldn't face her choosing me over you."

His eyes flared in pain as his voice changed to an agonized tone. "Damn it! *You* were there for her for the six fucking years I was in that hellhole. *You* stepped up and cared for her when you didn't have to. *You* helped her bring Trevor into this world and became a good father to him." Grant pointed toward the window and the main house across the yard. "*You* fell in love with her, and I don't blame you one damn bit." A tear rolled down his cheek as his voice broke. "I couldn't come back here and fuck that all up. I made my bed the day I signed on with the CIA, and I've spent every day, *every goddamn minute* of the past seven or eight years regretting it—not because of what I went through, but because of what I put you and Blair through. If you honestly believe I'm behind this whole fucking charade, then . . . then you're not the brother I used to know, and you certainly never knew me."

Without another word, he spun around and strode to the door, leaving them all behind. No one spoke. The only sound was the shuffling of feet. Drake was stunned by his sibling's admissions. Had he really just accused Grant of doing the unthinkable?

After a few moments, Shane moved into Drake's line of vision as he stared at the door Grant had disappeared through. Sympathy and understanding filled Shane's eyes. "He didn't deserve that, man. I get where you're coming from—I really do. But no matter what, I believe he had you and Blair and your family's best interest in mind when he decided not to let you know he was alive. He's not behind this mess."

Drake glanced around at the others, several of whom avoided his gaze before he found Shane's face again. Guilt riddled him, and he silently called himself a fucking fool. "I know—you're right. I'm sorry, everyone. I just . . ."

He couldn't find the words to explain his irrational accusation. He knew Grant better than anyone—even after all those years of separation. But instead of trusting his brother, Drake had let his fear and jealousy take over. He'd fucked up big time.

"We're not the ones you should be apologizing to," Price said solemnly.

He licked his lips, then nodded. "You're right."

When Shane stepped out of his way, Drake headed for the door, hoping he could repair the damage he'd just done.

Leaning against a fence post, Grant watched a rabbit nibble on the green leaves of a buried bunch of carrots in Blair's garden. The animal knew he was there, but after a few anxious movements, it seemed to realize the human wouldn't get any closer and went back to its meal. Grant could still recall his mother tending to her vegetables, which had been planted in the same fenced-in area—although the fence had been updated in the past year or so. When he'd been old enough, Susan Hadley had taught Grant how to prep the soil, seed and label the rows, and tend to the growing crops. The times he spent with his mother in the garden were some of his fondest memories of her.

Grant was torn between wanting to stay in Hazard, where he was miserable watching the woman he loved with his brother, or hightailing it out of there and disappearing again. The latter was impossible, at least until Blair, Drake, and the children were out of danger. He still hadn't told anyone but Lane, the police chief, and the special-ops guards that when he'd left Bar None the other day, there had been a live rattlesnake on the passenger seat of his locked SUV. Thankfully, the thing had been shaking its tail in warning before Grant had climbed in behind the steering wheel. It hadn't taken him long to use a long stick to get the damn thing out and carry it a few hundred yards into the woods behind the restaurant, where he'd bludgeoned it to death with a thick tree limb. He hadn't wanted it to return to the parking lot, where it would've been dangerous to any unsuspecting person walking by. It wasn't unheard of, every once in a while, for someone in the area to discover a snake in their vehicle, but Grant highly doubted this one had found its way into his SUV without assistance. Whoever was threatening his family was making sure Grant knew they were still out there, which meant, for now, he had to stay put.

"This is the third year Blair has planted vegetables in Mom's garden. She said it was a waste of space if she didn't do something with it." Drake stopped next to Grant and stared at the rabbit. "She'll be pissed when she finds out that thing got inside the wire fence again. I'm starting to think it's from the planet Krypton and can leap tall buildings in a single bound because I've tried everything to keep it out of there.

"You might want to talk to your daughter about that," Grant responded without looking at him. He was still angry and hurt by his brother's accusations but was trying to understand things from Drake's point of view. They'd been dancing around each other all week

—Blair too—and any conversation between them had been stilted and uncomfortable. They were like three strangers who were afraid to rock the boat—any more than it already was—by saying something that could evoke real emotions from the others. But at least Drake had sought him out after the ugly display in the workshop.

Grant pointed to one of the corner posts on the far side of the garden. "She was bending the bottom of the wire up over there when she thought no one was watching yesterday. I think she feels bad for the rabbit."

Bending at the waist, Drake eyed the fence section Grant was referring to. "Son of a . . . I should've known she'd do something like that. She kept talking about how the damn thing was the mother or father to a bunch of babies and had to feed them somehow. I think she'll be the vet or zoologist in the family or something along those lines."

They stood silently for several moments, staring at the nervous animal as it feasted, before Drake stuck his hands into the front pockets of his jeans and sighed. "I'm sorry, Grant. You called it—I was an asshole in there. I don't know what I was thinking and why I said what I said, but I don't believe it. I know you didn't send those pictures. But, damn it, this is uncharted territory for me. I've never been jealous of anyone since Blair and I grew close—she's never given me a reason to be. But here you are, the only other guy she's ever loved, and . . . and I don't want to lose her—not even to you."

"I don't blame you—she a helluva woman. Always was." Grant pursed his lips, wondering if he should say the words on the tip of his tongue. For the past few days, he'd been replaying his conversation with Tucker Wilson in his mind. After the two whiskeys Grant had downed, he'd refused the third Tuck had tried to order for him. As much as he'd wanted to get shit-faced at the time, he couldn't. He had his family to protect—Drake's family. But as he'd laid in bed later that night, he'd realized that Tuck hadn't just walked in there for a drink in the middle of the day and happened to find Grant at the bar. Nope, the man had sought him out. And that made Grant wonder if Tuck's husband, Shane, had visited Drake at some point to have a similar conversation with him. Whether he had or not, a seed had been planted in Grant's mind that afternoon, and it'd been trying to bloom ever since. But he was afraid to voice the idea of a ménage to Drake. It just might get Grant killed at the hands of his brother.

"I missed you, ya know." Drake's words came out in a whisper.

Grant reached out and squeezed his brother's shoulder. "I missed you too." It was true. When he hadn't been thinking about Blair or his tormentors during his time in captivity, he'd passed the long, lonesome days remembering all the good times he and Drake had experienced when they'd been younger. Losing their mother before they'd hit their teens had been hard, but Joe Hadley had done his best to give his sons some good memories despite his own grief. Fishing, hunting, and camping had been their favorite things to do together.

As the silence hung between them again, Grant was about to turn and say they should get back to the others, who were obviously still inside the workshop, but Drake's words stopped him dead in his tracks. "You didn't happen to talk to Shane or Tucker the other day, or any other day, did you? I don't mean about all that." He gestured toward his workshop as he continued to babble. "I mean, about . . . about us . . . you and I . . . giving Blair another option other than choosing between us. Did you and either of them talk about that?"

While trying to sort through the gibberish Drake had just spouted, a stunned Grant pivoted to face his brother, searching his expression for any signs he regretted the can of worms he'd opened. Had Grant heard him correctly? Was Drake talking about a ménage relationship with Blair? "Okay, call me a dumb schmuck if you want, but clarify that question for me. I don't want to say the wrong thing because I misunderstood what you said."

Taking a deep breath, Drake let it out slowly. "Sorry, most of that didn't make sense—not even to me. My question was . . . is . . . did Tucker or Shane talk to you about . . . you know . . . having a relationship like theirs?"

Grant chuckled as a grin spread across his face. "How are you going to do it if you can't even say the word, Drake? It's called a ménage or a threesome if that's what you're more comfortable with."

Shoving his hands into his hair, Drake huffed. "Damn it, you're not making this any easier. If someone suggested sharing Blair with another guy a week ago, I would've decked them. But . . . but after talking with Shane, the fucking manipulative bastard, I haven't been able to stop thinking about it. Not because I'm afraid she'll choose you, but because, together, we could care for her so much better than me or you alone. In more ways than one, if you know what I mean."

"I know what you mean. It never occurred to me either, but I know a few people in Tampa who have ménage relationships."

Drake gaped at him. "Seriously?"

He rolled his eyes. "Why does everyone keep asking me that? I'm serious ninety-nine percent of the time, yet everyone seems to need confirmation. Yes, seriously. I don't know them well—they're friends of friends—but I understand how it works. One threesome has two brothers who aren't into incest, so, logistically, the sex part of it can be done without any issues. I think after that, everything else should be easy. They both have alone time with their fiancée, since they travel at different times, and then they take care of her together. But, Drake, think about this long and hard. The last thing I want to do is come between you and Blair. And you have to think about how this town will respond to another ménage relationship in its mist."

His brother glanced away momentarily before looking him in the eyes again. "I know. And I've thought about it for days. While Blair has assured me that she'd never leave me, I can't help but think she'll be devastated if you walk out of her life again. I think we'll have to discuss a lot of things—put all the cards on the table. No secrets. No hiding our feelings, especially negative ones. We can't let there be any jealousy between us."

"Agreed."

"Agreed," Drake echoed. "As for the rest of the town, screw 'em. You, Blair, and the kids are the only ones who matter." He paused. "Okay, so how do we start this? How do we approach Blair?"

Grant shrugged his shoulders. "I haven't got a clue. You know her better than I do now, so what do you think? Will she even go for it?"

He snorted. "Shane suggested I check out her Kindle. Apparently, the reading club she's in really goes for ménage romance. Trust me when I say our Blair has a kinky side that even I didn't know about. One I'm looking forward to exploring."

Grant was shocked for a moment—more so from Drake saying "our" Blair than anything else—but then he threw his head back and laughed. "Well, okay then, little brother. I'll follow your lead for once in my life. But while you start cooking up a scheme to approach her about all this, let's get back inside so I can figure out who arranged our sudden family reunion." While giving Drake the lead, Grant wondered if his brother knew just how kinky Blair could get. They'd had some wild encounters during their relationship—but never involving bringing a third person into the mix.

Slapping Drake's shoulder, Grant shoved him toward the converted barn. For the first time since he'd heard Blair and Drake were married, Grant felt a glimmer of hope deep in his gut. Now, he just had to make sure no one extinguished it.

Chapter 14

Driving around the backroads on the outskirts of town, Grant tried to keep his mind on his mission—find whoever sent the photos and then gone silent, except for the snake—instead of on the conversation he'd had with Drake two days ago. While the brothers still hadn't figured out how to approach Blair about the relationship they wanted to try with her, the tension that'd always seemed to be in the room with the three of them had faded. Were he and Drake crazy thinking about sharing Blair? Would she even want to be shared by them? Or did she want Grant to return to Florida and leave them to live out their lives without him?

The morning after she'd slapped him across the face for being an asshole, Grant had apologized to her when he'd managed to get a moment alone with her in the kitchen. He'd been surprised when she asked if they could put it behind them. She'd said she was sorry for hitting him—even though he knew he deserved it—and even went up on her tiptoes and placed a platonic kiss on his cheek. Now, she seemed more relaxed, as if she was getting used to him being around again. The three adults were even falling into daily, benign routines that Blair and Drake already had but Grant now fitted into.

When he wasn't looking around Hazard Falls for someone from his past who wanted to hurt him, Blair, or Trevor, Grant was helping out around the house and property whenever and wherever he could. He'd even stepped up where the kids were concerned—playing catch with Trevor, reading a Winnie-the-Pooh story to Regan repeatedly, and making Michael laugh with simple magic tricks like pulling a quarter out of the boy's ear. While he'd started feeling more comfortable around everyone, Grant had been avoiding Drake's workshop. He'd already invaded his brother's house, so he hadn't wanted to do the same to his business. But now that they seemed to have buried the hatchet between them, he intended to see if he could help Drake with his work projects whenever he had free time. Grant may not be as talented as his brother regarding the fine nuances of woodworking, but he was experienced enough to assist him.

After eating lunch about an hour ago, Grant had gone out for one of the recon drives he took several times a day. He varied his routes and times of the day, ensuring he didn't conform to a routine that could be used against him. On this trip, he'd gone through the Liberty Campgrounds while talking on the phone with Nathan Cook in Tampa. Driving slowly past tents, RVs, campers, and a few double-wide trailers, Grant had rattled off the license plate of every vehicle he could find. The number had increased ten-fold in the past thirty-six hours, the last time he'd done this. He would also check for any new vehicles at the Moody Moon Motel. Since the rodeo started tomorrow, Cook already had several hundred in- and out-of-state plates to run from the campsites alone. Hopefully, he'd turn something up over the next few hours, but, in the meantime, Grant was still twiddling his thumbs, wondering what Drake would come up with on how they should approach Blair about a ménage.

Smiling, something Grant had rarely done over the past seven years, he tried to think of what Blair's shocked expression might be when she heard their proposal, but movement on the shoulder of the road, a short distance ahead of him, grabbed his attention. Grant slowed as a deer bolted across both lanes before disappearing into the woods. Thankfully, he'd had enough warning to avoid it. He could still remember the sound of impact when he struck a deer with the first pickup he'd ever bought at seventeen, after saving his money from summer jobs for two years. It'd been a beat-up Chevy, but the engine had been sound. At least, it had been until it met its demise after encountering a four-point buck. After that, the Hadley men had eaten venison for almost the entire winter, and Drake had mounted the antlers on a stained piece of wood as a gag trophy for his brother.

Grant had been surprised earlier when he'd noticed the antlers on the wall in Drake's workshop, having forgotten all about them until then. Hell, he'd forgotten many things from his youth that all seemed to rush back to him everywhere he turned. He hadn't realized how much he'd missed Hazard Falls. When he'd been a teen, he wanted nothing more than to leave the small town behind and make his mark in the world with Blairby his side. Now, he wished he'd listened to his father, brother, and friends when they'd tried to convince him to go into the construction business full-time and settle down in Hazard with Blair. Would they've been happy or regretted not following their dreams? Would they've had a big family by now? And where would that have left Drake? His brother would probably be married to someone else with a bunch of kids. Grant didn't like that idea for some reason—it gnawed at his gut. The more he thought about a ménage relationship with Blair and Drake, the more it felt right. Why should Grant go back to Tampa when his heart belonged here? There was nothing down there for him other than a sparsely furnished apart-ment, a few acquaintances, and his truck. No, he didn't belong in Florida. He belonged here—with Blair, Drake, Trevor, Regan, and Michael. Hell, he already loved all three kids as if he were their biological father instead of just Trevor's. Grant could have it all—his brother, the woman they both loved, and the children, including any more that came their way. Now, he just had to pray Blair was on board with the whole threesome thing and that Drake wouldn't regret his decision to try it. If it failed, Grant would have to be the one to bow out and go back to his non-existent life down south, and the thought of doing that threatened to rip his heart out.

Rounding a curve, Grant cursed when he saw a red pickup truck, about twenty feet off the opposite side of the road, sitting at an angle in a ditch, with steam coming from its damaged radiator. The bumper, hood, and headlights hadn't fared well either. A bloodied doe lay in the middle of the oncoming lane, not moving—someone else hadn't been as lucky as Grant had been moments earlier. No one else was around, so he had to pull over and ensure the driver was okay.

Grant passed the truck, did a quick U-turn, and then parked on the side of the road before putting the hazard lights on. If anyone came around the other bend in the road, they would hopefully have enough warning to slow down before hitting the deer.

Grabbing his gun from the middle console, where he'd put it for easy access if needed, Grant climbed out of the truck, tucking the weapon in the holster at his lower back and covering it with his shirt. If the animal were still alive, he'd put a bullet in its brain to keep it from suffering a painful death—he also didn't want to get caught without a gun if his unknown stalker showed up.

A quick glance at the deer as he strode past told him it was already dead—there was still no movement, and it wasn't breathing. He'd pull it to the side of the road after he checked on the driver. Turning his attention to the pickup truck, he approached the driver's door while taking off his sunglasses. The shade of the surrounding tall trees had made the dark lenses unnecessary.

Before he reached the door, an exasperated female voice came through the open window. "I'm fine, Albert, I swear, but the seatbelt is stuck, and I can't get out. Just call Josh and tell him to come out with the tow truck and a knife. Although, if you're already on your way, you'll probably beat him here."

Peeking into the truck's cab, Grant saw a blast from his past. Marla Oberman had owned the Stop & Go in Hazard, a combination grocery and general store, for about twenty years, having inherited it from her aunt and uncle, the original proprietors. It wasn't huge, but it saved many residents from driving forty minutes to the closest Walmart when they only needed a few basic things. Her husband ran the hardware store they'd moved from up the street to the shop next door to the Stop & Go. Al's Hardware & Gear also sold hunting, fishing, and camping equipment. There was even an indoor walkway between the two stores for easy access for the married couple and their patrons.

Grant eyed the gray-haired woman and noticed she had a small laceration on her forehead that was bleeding but not profusely. Otherwise, she appeared fine as she disconnected the call on her cell phone with a muttered curse.

"Are you okay?" Grant asked.

"Oh!" Her hand flew to her ample chest, and her wide-eyed gaze whipped to his. "Oh, sorry, I didn't realize anyone had stopped. Yes, I'm fine, I'm just—" Her face paled as she stared at him. "Oh, no, I'm not fine . . . nope, not fine at all. In fact, I'm hallucinating. Oh, Lord, that has to be it because I see a ghost. Tell me I'm not going out of my mind, Grant Hadley, because if I am, I'll need an ambulance, a straightjacket, and a rubber room, in that order." She looked him up and down, then shook her head. "I think you better add some whiskey in there to boot."

Shit. He should've left his sunglasses on. Of course, Marla would recognize him, even with the beard and mustache. She'd kept an eye on Grant and Drake those first few years after their mother had died before they'd been old enough to stay home alone after school until their father had gotten off work. During the summers, she'd filled in when needed, but many of their friends' parents had stepped in to help, too, inviting the brothers into their homes during the day. Grant remembered the weekly schedule they'd set up, so Joe Hadley hadn't needed to worry about his sons getting into trouble. That was the great thing about small towns—there were always people willing to lend a hand during tough times.

The last time he'd seen Marla had been a few months before Grant's ill-fated last assignment. Whenever Blair and Grant had visited Hazard a few times after moving permanently to D.C., they'd always made a point to stop in to see Marla and Al and treat them to lunch while their employees manned the stores.

Another vehicle, a green, four-door sedan, pulled to a stop next to the accident, and two other older women got out to see if they could help. Grant recognized them from the church he'd attended as a youth but couldn't recall their names off the top of his head, but they were two of the biggest gossips in town.

Setting his hands on the door, Grant sighed. He'd known, sooner or later, it would get out that he was back from the dead—it looked like that time was now. "No, you're not imagining things, Mrs. O. It's me."

"Oh, my Lord." Gaping at him, she tried to open the door, but the front quarter panel had been pushed back, blocking it. "Damn door. And this seatbelt is stuck too. Help me out of here, please, while I wrap my head around you not being dead and buried at sea."

Grabbing the handle, Grant yanked on it, and with some effort, he got it open just enough for him to squeeze in behind it and push it out further. When there was finally enough room for Marla to get out, he pulled out a pocketknife he always had on him and cut the strap holding her in place. Once free, she rotated in her seat until she faced him, then reached up and cupped his face with her hands. "It really is you. Oh, my Lord! Do Drake and Blair know?"

He gave her a small smile and gently grasped her wrists, pulling her hands away. "They do now." He retrieved a bandana he also kept in his back pocket. "Let me take a look at your forehead—you're bleeding."

"I am?" She touched her hand to her head and winced. "Oh, it's nothing. This old noggin has had worse."

"Marla, are you okay?" one of the old biddies called out from the roadway. She eyed Grant warily. "Who's that with you?"

Beside her, the other woman piped up. "That looks like Grant Hadley, doesn't it, Sue?"

"Isn't he dead?"

"I thought he was, but he doesn't look dead."

"Maybe he's one of those look-alikes that everyone supposedly has. What're they called again? Dope-gangers?"

As the two women discussed reincarnations and doppelgängers on the side of the road, Grant helped Marla from her incapacitated pickup. In the meantime, another vehicle, driven by Al Oberman, arrived moments before Lane pulled up in his patrol vehicle with its flashing lights on. Seconds later, a tow truck appeared with Josh Bennett, who was Grant's age, at the wheel—apparently, everyone had been nearby when the calls for help had come in. Grant was greeted by a new round of disbelief from the guy he'd gone to school with and Marla's husband. As he tried to explain to everyone but Lane that his reported death had been part of a classified mission with the Secret Service, the lawman grabbed the hind legs of the dead deer and dragged it out of the roadway.

It was a good fifteen minutes before Grant could finally disengage himself from the five people peppering him with questions he couldn't answer. Striding over to the police department's Chevy Tahoe, Grant stopped beside the driver's door. Lane was sitting inside, with the window rolled down, writing the accident report. He glanced at the little group, who were all pulling out their cell phones. "Twenty bucks says the whole town knows within the next five minutes."

Grant snorted. "I might've only been back to visit Hazard a few times since I went off to college, but I'm not stupid enough to take that bet. It was bound to happen—I'm actually surprised it took this long."

His cell phone rang, and he checked the screen before answering the call. "Hey, Nathan. What do you have for me?"

He could hear the geek tapping away on his computer's keyboard as he spoke. "I've got four parole violators, eleven separate warrants for domestic violence, a burglary, writing bad checks, grand larceny, shoplifting, and DWIs. I've got two dead-beat dads who skipped out on child support, six vehicles with revoked tags, one stolen vehicle, and a BOLO for a suspect in an assault in a bar last weekend. What I don't have is anyone I can connect to you, but with all this data, I could be missing something. I'll keep combing through it all. In the meantime, I'm sending everything the cops will probably want to check out to the email address I have for Chief Hughes. I'll send you and Price copies of that stuff and information on all the other registrations for you to review. Let me know if something stands out to you, and I'll follow up on it."

"Thanks, I appreciate it."

"No problem. Catch ya later."

Disconnecting the call, Grant turned back to Lane. "The bad news is Sawyer's man didn't find anything connecting anyone from the Liberty Campgrounds to me. The bad news is you'll probably be busy as hell later."

The cop groaned. "Let me guess—a bunch of tags came back with warrants."

"Among other things."

"Shit." He pulled on the door handle, and Grant stepped back to let him exit the vehicle. "I'm starting to hate that damn rodeo."

Grant didn't blame him, but he had other stuff on his mind. "If you don't need me for anything, I'm heading back to the house. We're probably gonna have our own shit to deal with as the gossip mill's phones start to heat up. See you later."

"Later."

As Grant walked toward his rental, Marla intercepted him. She waved his now-bloodied bandana at him. "Thank you for stopping, Grant. I'll get this back to you as soon as I wash it."

"You don't have—"

"Oh, hush." She reached out and took his hand, squeezing it. "I know you can't tell us what really happened to you, but I want you to know you're always welcome in Hazard. We missed you—you're family to many people here, whether you realize it or not. And if you need anything, just let Albert or me know, and we'll be there."

Leaning down, he gave her a peck on the cheek. "Thanks, Mrs. O."

She clicked her tongue. "You're old enough to call me Marla. Now, go do whatever you have to do, and thank you again for stopping to help."

"I'm glad I was in the right place at the right time."

With a final squeeze, she let go of his hand. As he started for his vehicle again, Grant thought of the list of reasons he'd made as a teen about why he'd wanted to leave Hazard Falls and realized it didn't compare to the list of what he'd left behind.

Chapter 15

Blair was loading the dishwasher with the empty plates and glasses from the kids' lunches when the house phone rang. After quickly wiping her hands on a dish towel, she grabbed the cordless receiver from its cradle on the wall. "Hello?"

"Hey, Blair, it's Nicole. Just calling to make sure you're okay."

Her eyes narrowed at the concern in her friend's voice as she hung the towel on the oven handle. "Hi . . . um, I'm fine . . . why wouldn't I be?"

"Oh, good, I'm the first one to call. Get ready for the floodgates to open. Apparently, the cat's out of the bag, and the gossip mill knows about Grant."

Walking into the family room where Regan and Michael played with their toys, Blair sat on the sofa's edge. "What do you mean? What happened? Is he okay?"

"He's fine, but Marla Oberman hit a deer on Shadow Rock Road, and Grant was the first one there."

"Oh, no! Is she hurt?" Marla was one of the sweetest women in Hazard Falls, and Blair hoped she wasn't badly injured. There'd been more than one fatal accident involving deer over the years on that road, but speed was usually a contributing factor in those cases.

"From what I heard, she banged her head a bit, messed up the front of her truck, and killed the deer, but other than that, she's okay. She didn't even go to the clinic or emergency room. She was more shaken up about Grant, thinking she was hallucinating at first."

"She wasn't the only one," Blair admitted. "I still do a double take every time he walks into the room." That was true—she kept thinking it was one of her dreams of him and expected to awaken at any moment to find out none of it was real. "Grant didn't ask her to stay quiet? I mean, I know Marla loves to chat, but she's also good about keeping secrets when necessary."

"I'm sure he didn't have a chance to ask her before Sue Pinsky and Benita Ross stopped to help not long after he did. There's no way those two can resist burning up the cell towers with juicy gossip. Then Albert arrived, and a few minutes later, Josh showed up with the tow truck. Expect a lot of calls and a few gawkers driving by, trying to get a glimpse of the prodigal son of Hazard."

Blair sighed as her cell phone rang in the kitchen, and the cordless in her hand beeped, signaling a call-waiting simultaneously. After checking the number, she ignored the call on the house line. "I think it's starting already. Thanks for the heads up. I'll call you back later."

The back door opened, and she heard Drake walk in while talking on his phone, with Roscoe on his heels. The dog passed through the kitchen and ran upstairs, probably heading for Trevor's bedroom. Drake's voice filtered into the family room. "Yes, Pastor Harrington, it's true . . . yes, it's a miracle . . . no, I'm sorry, I'm not at liberty to say where he's been all this time . . . no, he wasn't trying to deceive anyone . . . yes, sir . . . no, sir . . . I will, sir. Goodbye, Pastor."

When he disconnected the call, his phone rang again as Blair met him in the kitchen. She rolled her eyes as her cell's ringtone joined his, followed by the cordless phone in her hand again. She glanced at the screen and didn't answer the call. It was one of the church ladies calling. Instead, Blair turned off the ringer. Drake did the same after declining to accept the call on his cell.

Blair checked the incoming number on her iPhone and chose to answer that call. "Hi, Paige. Yes, I'm fine, but the phones are ringing off the hook, and I only found out about Marla from Nicole two seconds ago. Grant isn't back yet, but I'm sure he's on his way. Drake is here, and we're screening our calls."

Her friend chuckled. "Well, damn, girl. I like it when I don't have to play twenty questions with you. You covered everything I was going to ask except one thing —do you need us to help you with the kids or anything?"

She eyed Drake, who apparently was getting text messages now that he wasn't answering his phone. "Thanks, Paige, but I don't think so. I'll call you if we do. I have a feeling we'll be holed up here for the next twenty-four to forty-eight hours, at least, until things calm down again."

"Well, then, let me send dinner over with Shane. He's stopping at Bar None with Ari after they run a few errands. I'll have them make you a few pizzas unless you want something else."

Leaning against the counter, Blair rubbed her temples. "That would be fantastic—tell Shane I'll pay him when he gets here."

"Oh, hush. It's on us tonight. You've got enough to deal with without trying to remember where you put your purse."

Blair couldn't hold back the laughter that erupted from her, and some of the tension she hadn't known was there left her neck and shoulders. It was a standing joke among her friends that she forgot where she put her damn bag on a regular basis. She was starting to think the kids moved it to drive her nuts and send her hunting for it in every room. It just never seemed to be where she thought she'd left it. "Thank you. We'll treat you next time."

"No worries. Let me call it in. Just cheese on one pie

and pepperoni on another, right? Will that be enough with Grant there?" The bar pies weren't as large as the ones from the pizzeria on the other side of town, but the crust and sauce tasted far better, in Blair's opinion. Paige's family agreed with her.

The front door swung open, and Grant strode in with two of the men who'd been watching the property and her family. This was the first time more than one of them had been in the house simultaneously, and it was probably because the word of Grant's presence in Hazard was no longer a secret. She might as well feed them while they were here. "Actually, can you make it two pepperoni and two cheese? Two of the guards are here and probably will be for a while." When Paige said it was no problem, Blair wrapped up the call. "Thanks. I'll talk to you later."

Grant entered the kitchen with the two men—Vic, the retired SEAL, and Manny Cortez, whom she'd been told had been a Marine Raider. With the four huge male bodies in the room, Blair felt petite, something that hadn't happened since before her first pregnancy. She was grateful when they all took seats at the table. "Is Marla okay, Grant?"

"Yeah, she's fine. I think she was more freaked out about me than the damage to her truck or the laceration on her forehead. It didn't look like she needed stitches, though." He gestured to the two men whose physiques looked like they were still in the special forces. "Victor, Manny, and the others will no longer be hiding, but we'll pass them off as friends of mine if anyone asks. With the entire town knowing I'm alive by now, we may have people showing up on our doorsteps. The guards won't be able to tell who's friendly from a distance, and we can't risk that. I know some people won't believe they're just visiting, but I don't give a rat's ass. I get the feeling we'll be hearing from our photographer soon."

When Drake's eyes narrowed at that statement, Grant explained, "Call it a hunch. Whoever it is was waiting for us to get complacent, and that's another reason why I want the guards visible. New guys will be arriving tonight. Those are the ones who will be monitoring things from a distance now. If this guy has been watching, he may know we've had protection. If he sees Vic, Manny, Bruce, and Liam staying close to the house, he might miss the new guys and accidentally make himself known." Bruce Whitfield and Liam Hennessy were the other former military men guarding the Hadleys.

"I wish we could take the children somewhere safe," Blair said. "But I have no idea where to take them. Do you really think this guy might harm them?"

Grant stood, and Blair was shocked but relieved when he pulled her into his arms and held her gently against his hard chest. The act felt comforting and natural, as if no time had passed since they'd said goodbye when she'd dropped him off at the airport all those years ago. Drake was behind Grant so that she couldn't see her husband's reaction to his brother holding his wife, but Blair hoped he wasn't jealous or hurt. Right then, she needed Grant's strength, expertise, and knowledge about the situation. Drake knew nothing about the world of secret agents and special-ops people. He knew carpentry, raising and protecting his family, and the normal, everyday stuff most Midwesterners dealt with daily. The residents of Hazard Falls had experienced their fair share of rough times over the years—droughts, tornados, house fires, etc.—and Drake stepped up to help whenever he could. But the CIA? Black-ops teams? International intrigue and espionage? Stalkers? Yeah, those were Grant's specialties, apparently.

God, she was still trying to wrap her head around that. Her Grant—a US spy. She never suspected he hadn't been working with the Secret Service, guarding some diplomat's life in a foreign country. He'd always been smart, figuring things out faster than anyone else she ever knew, so now that she was aware of what he'd really been doing back then, it wasn't such a ridiculous thought. Even though he'd been caught, he'd probably been very good at his job. Blair still wondered how that'd happened because she couldn't see Grant being outwitted by someone else.

Grant's warmth infused itself into Blair's body, pushing down the chill she felt whenever she thought of her family being in danger. His hands rubbed her back as he held her, and she tried to ignore the way her nipples pebbled or the stirring she felt in her core. Even after all these years, her body recognized his. It'd been several days since Tucker and Shane had spoken to the Hadley brothers. Blair had resigned herself to the fact that neither Drake nor Grant was interested in a ménage relationship since neither had mentioned a word of it. At least she knew without either of them knowing how much she wanted both of them. She would have to keep that to herself because she never wanted Drake to feel like she'd settled for him due to their marriage certificate. If she had to choose, she'd choose her husband every time. That didn't mean she wouldn't love both men equally in her heart.

With her head resting on Grant's chest, she felt and heard each word he spoke. "No, I don't think he'll go after the children, sweetheart. He wants me, and he's using the threat to my family for his own twisted reasons. As soon as I know what they are, I'll use them to bring him down. Drake, the guards, and I won't let anything happen to you or the kids. I swear it. I'll bring hell to Hazard before letting anything happen to you."

As if suddenly realizing how their embrace might look to the other men in the room, specifically Drake, Grant released her and stepped back. Her body shivered at the loss of contact. Not wanting to see the look on Drake's face, Blair took the coward's way out. "Um, okay. Let me check on the children while y'all . . . do whatever it is you need to do."

She hurried from the room and up the stairs.

Trevor was in his bedroom, where he occasionally locked himself in whenever he needed a break from his siblings pestering him. However, before Blair knocked on his door, she detoured into the master bedroom. Her body was flushed with arousal—arousal for a man who wasn't her husband, whom she loved with all her heart. Guilt-filled tears poured from her eyes. Heaven help her, she was in love with two men. Thankfully, her friendship with Paige, and the one she'd had with Sarah, Shane and Tucker's first wife, meant loving two men wasn't a foreign idea, but it was one Blair had never had before.

Neither Grant nor Drake indicated they'd spoken to Tucker and Shane. Maybe they didn't want to share her. Maybe Drake wanted his brother to leave. Maybe Grant wanted to leave the moment the danger to her family no longer existed. Would she survive losing Grant again, knowing, this time, it would be his own choice?

Chapter 16

Through the kitchen doorway, Drake regarded the stairs leading to the second-floor bedrooms. Blair had run up them about fifteen minutes ago and still hadn't returned. At first, a pang of jealousy had stabbed him when Grant had taken Blair into his arms to comfort her. But then his brother had pivoted slightly, and Drake had seen Blair's shoulders relax as Grant had told her she and the kids were safe and he'd make sure they stayed that way.

That's when it hit Drake. Shane had been right. The two brothers combined could give Blair everything she needed, including their love and support. They could do this, Drake was sure of it now, as long as Blair was willing to try it. God, he wished she'd give him a sign— a glaring one—so he didn't assume something she didn't want.

As Grant, Vic, and Manny discussed the new guard

schedule, Drake stepped into the family room to check on Regan and Michael, who were coloring and playing with Legos, respectively. "How are you doing, kids?"

Michael just shrugged, but Regan looked up at her dad. "I'm hungry—what's for dinner?"

"Uncle Shane is dropping off pizza in a little bit." Drake had gathered that much from Blair's conversation with Paige.

"Yay! Is Ari coming too?"

"I don't know, pumpkin, but if she is, she's not staying for dinner tonight. Maybe next time." Any other time, he would've invited the young girl he considered a niece to dinner, but not with the possible danger to the Hadleys lurking out there.

Regan sighed as if Drake had just crushed her dreams. "All right." But then she smiled, hopefully. "Is Uncle Grant eating with us again tonight?"

Taking a seat on the couch next to where his daughter was kneeling on the floor in front of the coffee table, Drake stroked her head. "Yeah, he is. Is that okay with you?"

She nodded. "Uh-huh. I like Uncle Grant. I wish he could live with us all the time. He makes funny voices when he reads me stories, and he's gonna teach me some tricks, like taking a quarter out of Michael's ear. I think it would be fun to have two dads like Ari has."

Hmm—out of the mouths of babes. Drake's kids had been around Shane, Tuck, and Paige so much that it didn't seem odd to them that Ari and Ashley had two fathers. As far as Drake knew, Ari didn't suffer any bullying at school because of her parents' unconventional marriage. However, that might change as she grew older and her peers noticed the Wilsons were out of the norm and started hearing the snide comments from some of their own parents who gossiped about the trio.

Drake was saved from responding to Regan's wish when the doorbell rang. She jumped up and ran for the front door before he could stop her. "I'll get it!"

He hurried after her. "Regan, no, I'll get it."

Thankfully, Vic had come from the kitchen and beat her to the door. "Hang on, squirt. Let me see who it is first, and then you can open the door."

"Okay, Mister Vic." As far as the children knew, the man who stopped in occasionally was Grant's friend.

As the little girl waited somewhat impatiently, Vic peered out the small peephole, unlocked the door, and stepped back. "All right, you can open it."

Regan didn't hesitate to do just that. "Hi, Uncle Shane! Hi, Ari!"

The father and daughter duo stood on the porch, carrying four pizzas between them. Regan opened the screen door for them to enter. Drake accepted the flat box Ari held out to him before taking the other three from Shane. "Thanks for grabbing us dinner."

Shane shrugged. "No problem. The phones still ringing like crazy?"

"Don't know. We shut off the landline and muted the cells."

"I don't blame you one bit." After glancing at the two girls chatting away and the retreating back of Vic heading back toward the kitchen, Shane leaned in and lowered his voice. "How are things going with you, Grant, and Blair?" He waggled his eyebrows.

Drake couldn't help the smile that spread across his face. "You're nosier than half the old bats in town, ya know that?"

"Of course I know that. But the difference between them and me is I can keep my mouth shut."

"After you tell Paige and Tucker."

"Right," Shane responded with a snort. "After I tell them—and you still didn't answer my question."

Drake peeked up the staircase to ensure Blair wasn't standing there before facing his friend again. "Grant and I are on board, but we're unsure how to approach Blair with the idea."

"That's easy—seduce her in the kitchen after the kids go to bed, and let Grant . . ." He made air quotes. ". . . accidentally walk in and become a voyeur. I'll bet you a hundred bucks Blair gets turned on even more when she realizes he's watching."

"But what if she's not?"

Shane rolled his eyes. "Dude, why do you think Tuck and I talked to you and Grant about this? Jeez, you're slow on the uptake here. She talked to Paige. Paige talked to me and Tuck. Blair loves you both, you dumb a—" He cut off the last word when his eyes shifted to the nearby girls, even though they didn't seem to be paying attention to their fathers. "And she doesn't want to lose either of you."

Drake's eyes went wide. "Seriously? She said that?"

"Not in those exact words, but yeah. I know she loves you, Drake, but she also never stopped loving Grant. Don't make her choose because, either way, she'll have to give up a man she loves, which will hurt her more than anything. So, man up and seduce the hell out of her. Trust me, it'll be worth it."

Shane was nothing but blunt. However, this was one of those times when Drake appreciated the fact. With only a moment's hesitation, Drake nodded. "All right, we'll give it a shot."

His friend clapped him on the shoulder. "Good. Now that that's decided, do you need anything else?"

Lifting the pizza boxes he was still holding, Drake shook his head. "No, this was more than enough. Thanks."

"No problem. Ari, let's go, sweetheart. We've got to get home with our dinner before Papa starts growling like a hungry bear."

After making sure Regan locked the door after Shane and Ari left, Drake carried the pizzas into the kitchen and noticed Michael had joined the men there, showing them his favorite John Deere toy tractor. Drake set the boxes down on the table. "Hey, Regan, sweetie, run upstairs and tell Mommy and Trevor dinner's here."

"Okay." She skipped toward the stairs. "Mommy! Trevor! Dinner's here!"

"I think she missed the 'run upstairs' part." Grant chuckled as he grabbed plates from the cabinets and handed them to Vic.

"My daughter's the same way," the retired SEAL responded. "Takes the shortcut any time she can."

Grant raised an eyebrow at him. "I didn't know you had kids."

The man nodded. "Just one—she lives with her mother in Texas. We're divorced. I only get to see Chrissy once a month and a few weeks during the summer."

Drake felt sorry for the man. He couldn't imagine not seeing Trevor, Regan, and Michael every day, watching them grow and not missing a minute of their young lives. He glanced at his brother and vowed Grant wouldn't have to miss a minute of Trevor's life from now on. If anything ever happened to Drake, he wanted to know, without a doubt, that his family would be cared for by his brother like Drake had taken over the care of Grant's family seven years ago.

When Blair walked into the busy kitchen, looking as beautiful as always, Drake decided tonight was the night the Hadley brothers would start seducing the woman they loved.

AFTER PIZZA, ITALIAN ICES, AND A DISNEY MOVIE, Grant volunteered to tuck the kids into bed while Drake and Blair cleaned the kitchen and family room. The guards had left to get some sleep before taking their respective watch details. Blair had enjoyed Vic and Manny's company. She'd been surprised to hear that Manny had grown up in Baltimore while Vic had been raised in the suburbs of Los Angeles because both men seemed very comfortable with small-town life. Vic explained that while he'd spent a few summers on his aunt and uncle's ranch in Montana, the military community also had a small-town feel. Everyone had their team members' backs and vice versa. When they were home, near whichever base they were stationed at, backyard barbecues and other get-togethers were common. The beer, food, laughter, and gossip flowed, just like it did in Hazard Falls whenever there was something to celebrate or when someone had a party just for the hell of it. Blair hadn't realized how alike the two communities were. She guessed it made sense after hearing stories about how the spouses of those in the military were always there for each other during long deployments.

Blair handed Drake the last glass, then pulled the

plugs in both sink sections to let the water drain. As she ran the sponge along the rims of the basins and the faucets, Drake stepped behind her and clutched her hips. Blair stilled and almost moaned when he rubbed his thick erection against her ass. This was the first time since the night Grant had returned that Drake had touched her like this, and she sighed in relief. She hadn't wanted to push him, knowing he'd have to come to terms with the presence of the man she'd once loved more than anyone else on Earth. The man she was still in love with, although she couldn't admit that to either Hadley brother. Not until she was certain it wouldn't hurt Drake and make him think she loved Grant more than him. She didn't.

God, she'd never understood how Paige had lost her heart to two men until now. Yeah, it happened all the time in the ménage books they read, but she'd always thought real life was far different. Thank goodness for Paige and her husbands—otherwise, Blair would have thought something was wrong with her, falling for the brothers and wanting them both. If only they'd give her a hint that they wanted the same thing she did. Neither had mentioned or had given any indication that Shane and Tucker had spoken to them about a threesome relationship, and she was terrified to bring up the subject on her own. But she was also terrified that when the danger to her and the children was gone, Grant would disappear from her life again. Blair didn't think she'd survive that happening a second time.

Drake's hands slid up her sides and then moved to cup her breasts. He nuzzled the bare column of her neck and bit down lightly, and Blair couldn't suppress the moan that escaped her. She could feel her husband's smile against her skin. "You like it when I nibble on you, don't you?"

"Yes." That single word was said on a breathy exhale. She reached back and grasped his ass as he tucked one hand into the V-neck of her shirt and under her bra. Her eyes fluttered shut when he rolled her nipple between his thumb and forefinger. Desire flooded her core, and she tried to remember the last time they'd had sex outside the bedroom. As the kids had grown, it had become harder to have stolen moments and quickies that wouldn't be interrupted by calls for Mommy and Daddy. It was one of the few reasons she couldn't wait until all three were in school.

Drake's pelvis moved and rocked against her buttocks, and memories assaulted Blair. Drake had never expressed interest in anal sex, so she'd always assumed it wasn't his thing. But it had definitely been his brother's thing. Grant had loved taking Blair anywhere he could—her mouth, pussy, and ass had all been filled with him at one time or another. Hell, if the man could've figured out a way to fuck her ear and belly button, she was sure he would've done it—and she would have let him.

It wasn't that sex with Drake was dull or not on par with Grant, it was just different. She'd never brought the things she'd done with Grant into the bedroom with her husband. Drake had known the only other man she'd ever slept with had been Grant, and she'd never wanted him to think she was comparing the two of them. But, right now, she kind of wished she'd let him know that she enjoyed anal sex. It wasn't for all women, but Blair missed it. Whenever Grant had taken her ass, he'd filled her pussy with a vibrator and fucked her with it and his cock at the same time. What would it be like if Grant was in her ass while she rode Drake's shaft? The thought had her racing toward an orgasm, and Drake was still only playing with her tits. He hadn't touched her throbbing clit yet, but she was ready to go off like a rocket the moment he did.

While she was totally into what Drake did to her, Blair suddenly felt they weren't alone. Her eyes opened and shifted to the left, and she gasped. Grant was leaning against the doorframe leading to the hall, staring at her and Drake. His eyes were heavy with lust, and there was no mistaking the bulge in the crotch of his jeans. The way his arms were crossed over his chest made the muscles of his shoulders and biceps more deliciously defined. The man was still sex on two legs. Both Hadley men were.

Blair was shocked when, instead of backing away from her at the intrusion, Drake turned her until she faced his brother. His hand remained down her shirt, and his cock still nestled against her ass. Drake's mouth found her ear and licked it. His voice was raspy and sensual as he murmured, "He wants you, baby. Just as much as I do. If you want him to join us, just ask him to."

Her mouth dropped open, and Grant's chuckle was low and rumbling as his gaze lifted from where Drake was teasing her nipple to her face. "Damn, she's still the prettiest woman I've ever seen when she blushes."

Holy hell, she must be dreaming. She was standing in her kitchen with the two most alluring men she'd ever known, and they both wanted her—together! Right? *Oh, please, let me be right.*

She squeaked when Drake nipped her ear. "If this isn't what you want, tell us, baby. Grant and I talked. We're both on board with giving you what we think you want and need. No jealousy. No regrets. We both just want to love you."

Oh, she definitely craved that, too, but needed to clarify a few things first. "I—are you . . ." She took a deep breath and let it out slowly, trying to calm her nerves. She eyed Grant. "I-I want this, but not if you'll leave after you find whoever sent those photos. This is all or nothing, Grant. I love Drake with all my heart but never stopped loving you. To—to be able to love you both at the same time—I never thought it was possible, but I was wrong. My love isn't split between the two of you—each of you getting a share—it encompasses both of you and the children. You all belong to me, to my heart. I couldn't take it if this . . . this threesome is only temporary. I know we'll have a lot to work out, but if

Shane, Tuck, and Paige can do it, I think we can too. But I need to know you're staying." Before he could answer, she turned in Drake's arms to look at him. "And I need to hear you tell me again that you won't regret this. I need to see your face when you say it. You're not doing this because you're afraid of losing me, are you? Because you won't."

Drake cupped her jaw, then leaned down and kissed her sweetly on her mouth. She saw the truth in his eyes when he lifted his head again. They were filled with love, trust, and understanding. "No, I'm not. I'm doing this because I love you, and I'm afraid of *you* losing *me* someday. If something happens to me, I know Grant will be here for you and the kids. I'm doing this because I can't think of anyone else on this earth I'd even consider sharing you with other than my brother. I'm doing this so you don't have to choose between the two men you love. I don't know why I was fighting the idea at first because I already knew you'd never stopped loving him—I've always known that—but it never made a difference in how much you loved me too. You were right when you said we'd have a lot to figure out about being in a ménage relationship since this is so new to all of us, but I have faith in you and Grant that we'll make this work. We'll both need our alone time with you, but most of the time, it'll be like this when Grant and I come to you together."

Her heart swelled with love for her husband. She'd been afraid of his response more than Grant's, but he'd quickly and efficiently quelled her fears. She placed a kiss on his lips. "I love you, always."

The corners of his mouth pulled upward. "I know you do, sweetheart, and I'll always know that."

Turning back to Grant, Blair met his gaze. "Well?"

Pushing off the doorframe, he strode toward her—actually, stalked was a more appropriate word—and cupped her chin. "I'm an ass for staying away from you both for so long. It never occurred to me we could work this out where no one had to choose, and I didn't want to hurt either of you. I won't lie—I tried to banish you from my memories by sleeping with a few women in Florida—but it never worked and just frustrated me even more that I couldn't have you. None of them meant a thing to me other than a few hours of sexual release. It was never in my bed, I never lied to any of them about it being more than a one-night-stand, I never stayed the night, and I always used a condom."

Blair tried not to let the thought of Grant with other women hurt her. She knew that wasn't the reason he'd told her. They'd never had secrets between them—well, except what his job had entailed—and she would've been more upset if he hadn't been upfront about his short-lived affairs. She had to be understanding about it, considering she'd married his brother. Grant had thought his relationship with her was over, and she couldn't expect him to be a monk for the rest of his life if he didn't think he could be with her again. All that was in the past, and now was their time to start their future—together.

"My heart has always belonged to you, Blair. There hasn't been a single night in seven years that I didn't fall asleep with visions of you in my head." He swallowed hard, and his voice broke. "If you'll have me, I'll stay."

Tears filled Blair's eyes as she went up on her tiptoes and wrapped her arms around Grant's neck. She pulled him close and kissed him the way she'd wanted to ever since he'd walked back into their lives. Grant moaned and closed the last bit of distance between them, pressing his chest against the nipples Drake had left throbbing with need. His tongue swept into her mouth and danced with hers. The intense passion she'd felt with Drake moments before came rushing back.

Not wanting Drake to feel left out, Blair dropped one arm and reached back, grabbing his hip and urging him closer. She wanted to feel sandwiched between them. Drake's hard-on rubbed against her butt cheeks again, and she moaned at the contact. Drake dragged her hair aside, giving him access to her neck again. He nibbled on her soft skin before whispering, "I never thought I'd be turned on by watching someone else kiss you, but damn, that's hot."

His hips tilted, and he humped her ass, pushing her into Grant's thick erection. Drake grasped her T-shirt at her waist and pulled it out of her jeans. He didn't stop lifting it until he'd exposed her chest. "Grant, take a breather for a sec."

Grant ended the kiss with obvious reluctance so Drake could draw the shirt over Blair's head. Her heart rate raced as Grant stared at her bra-restricted breasts. Slowly bringing his hands up, he cupped the orbs and raised them as if testing their weight and recalling all the times he'd worshiped them. Blair wondered if he was displeased with her breasts now—the last time he'd seen them was before she'd given birth to and nursed three children.

"Hey, what was that thought?"

She hadn't realized she'd stiffened and frowned at the idea Grant wouldn't like her body now. At Grant's question, Drake stepped around her and stood beside his brother with concern in his eyes. "Blair?"

Staring at her husband's chest, she shrugged. "My body's different from the last time Grant saw me. I don't want him to be disappointed."

"Aw, sweetheart, look at me," Grant ordered as he cupped her jaw. She hesitated before meeting his gaze. "You could never disappoint me. You're still the most beautiful woman I've ever known. And these curves?" He ran his hands down her sides and over her wide hips. "They just make you even sexier than the last time I saw you—especially knowing they're the result of three beautiful kids, one of whom is mine." He clutched her hips and pulled her toward him. "I'm looking forward to holding onto these as I fuck your ass. God, I miss that almost as much as I miss being inside your pussy."

Blair's mouth dropped open, and she didn't want to look at Drake. He had to be shocked by Grant's blunt announcement. Apparently, Grant caught a glimpse of his brother's astonished face because he asked, "What's wrong, Drake?"

"Um . . . you . . . you—you two had . . . um . . . a-anal sex? Blair?"

Obviously, he didn't want to hear the answer from his brother—he wanted it from her. Blair's cheeks flamed as she kept her gaze on his chest, but his hand reached out and tilted her chin until her only choice was to close her eyes or look at his intense gaze.

Oh boy.

Chapter 17

Grant looked back and forth between his brother and the woman they both loved. Either Blair had lied to him all those years ago when she'd told him she loved anal sex, or she'd hidden the fact from Drake. Grant was inclined to go with the latter. His Blair had been as voracious about sex as he'd been. He was pretty sure they'd done about three-quarters of the Kama Sutra positions back then and probably would've tried them all by now if he hadn't ended up in that damn prison camp.

If he didn't take over this conversation, he might be taking another cold shower tonight—and that wasn't happening. Not after he'd kissed Blair and couldn't wait to do it again. Thinking about Carter, Sawyer, and the other men who belonged to Sawyer's BDSM club in Tampa, Grant channeled his inner Dominant.

He frowned, took a step back, and crossed his arms. "I get the impression there are things you two never discussed concerning your sex life. I'm not sure why, but that ends right here and now. Blair, Drake asked you a question—you owe him a truthful answer. If this is going to work between the three of us, communication is going to be key."

Blair's throat rippled as she swallowed hard before her eyes met Drake's. "I'm sorry. You never expressed any interest in that, and I didn't want you to think I was comparing you to Grant."

Groaning, Drake thrust his hands into his hair. "And I didn't think you'd be interested either. We'd taken things so slowly in the beginning, everything vanilla, and I was afraid I'd scare you if I told you some of my fantasies. Sex was always great between us, you rock my world all the time, but I thought I'd embarrass you and turn you off by asking for anal. Now I'm kicking myself in the ass—no pun intended—for not being open about things I wanted to do to you—with you."

"I think you'll find Blair will like most of those things, brother." Grant smirked. "Is there anything else you two need to discuss, or can we move this into the master bedroom? If I don't get out of these jeans soon, I'll have a permanent indent from the button fly."

Drake chuckled and pulled Blair into his arms, kissing her forehead. "We can't let that happen, can we, honey? Besides, I agree with him. Lead the way, so I can eye that gorgeous ass that I can't stop thinking about now."

She blushed and smiled but did as requested and, without bothering to put her shirt back on, led them down the hall to the master bedroom. Thank God it was on the opposite side of the house from the kids' rooms on the second floor. Grant planned to do nasty, delicious things to their mother that they didn't need to wake up and hear. He realized now that he'd never heard his parents going at it all those years ago—not that he had ever wanted to.

As they followed Blair, both Drake's and Grant's gazes were glued to her shapely ass, and Grant's mouth watered. Even though he'd been jacking off every day to mental images of her ever since arriving in Hazard, he was certain he wouldn't last more than a minute inside her body before exploding like a randy teenager losing his virginity. Drake would, undoubtedly, ensure Blair was taken care of the first time, and Grant would just have to make it up to her in round two—and round three.

Once they were behind the closed bedroom door, Blair turned to face them. A flash of uncertainty appeared on her face. "I—um—how do we start this?"

Grant grinned suggestively. "Oh, we've already started, sweetheart, but before we continue, I want to watch Drake undress you—slowly."

GRANT LEANED BACK AGAINST THE WALL AND CROSSED his arms and ankles. His body might seem relaxed, but his dark eyes told a different story. He was strung tightly and trying not to pounce on her. Blair looked forward to testing his restraint. Her mouth turned up in a sexy smile as she pivoted toward Drake and kicked off her slippers. "You heard the man."

"I most certainly did." Drake didn't go straight to stripping her. Instead, he took measured steps as he circled around her. His hand trailed at an excruciatingly slow pace up her arm, across her bare back, and around to the front, just under her breasts. Goosebumps followed wherever he touched her, and Blair shivered in anticipation. Yes, sex with Drake had been more on the vanilla side over the years when compared to sex with Grant, but her husband had no trouble giving her amazing orgasms. Their styles might differ, but Grant and Drake knew how to please their woman, and now, Blair would have both of them pleasing her simultaneously. The combination might just kill her or, at least, put her into a sex-induced coma.

Drake stopped behind her and unhooked her lacy bra. Her breasts dropped to their natural state, and she wavered again at the thought of Grant being disappointed in the maternal changes to her body. Sliding the straps down, her husband revealed the fleshy orbs to his brother. Grant's eyes heated again, and he gulped but didn't move or say a word. His reaction brought her confidence back up a few notches. Remembering how he loved to watch her play with her nipples, she brought her hands up and tugged on them, which made her clit throb even more. She knew her actions had gotten the intended response when Grant uncrossed his ankles and unashamedly adjusted the bulge in his crotch.

Reaching around her waist, Drake unsnapped her jeans and lowered the zipper. Blair was wet and wanting as her gaze remained on Grant. Drake peeled off her jeans, and she stepped out of them. Now, the only thing she had on was her panties, and her men were both fully dressed. That knowledge ratcheted up her desire.

Blair licked her suddenly dry lips and waited for Grant to say something. His fiery gaze dragged upward from her feet to her torso. After lingering a few moments on her breasts, his eyes reached her face. "I hope those aren't a favorite pair of panties."

Oh, God! She knew what he was about to do before he even stepped toward her. When they'd been together, she'd lost numerous pieces of underwear when he'd ripped them off her in a whirlwind of passion.

She stood perfectly still as he approached. The

corners of his mouth ticked upward, and there was a hint of laughter in his eyes—he knew what she was remembering. Blair smiled smugly and didn't protest when he grabbed the waistband of the lacy garment and shredded it from her body. He brought the ruined fabric to his nose and inhaled her scent. His eyes practically rolled back in his head as he hummed. "Mmm, just as tantalizing as I remember."

Dropping the panties to the floor, Grant tugged her hand, leading her toward the bed. He sat down and pulled her between his knees. "I need to feast on that delicious pussy of yours that I've been dreaming about while Drake fucks your mouth. Brother, what do you think her punishment should be if she comes before you do?"

"Punishment? Hmm, I like the sound of that," Drake responded in her ear. She jumped because she hadn't known he'd moved with her and Grant. He held her still by grasping her hips. "How about a spanking, sweetheart? Is that something else Grant used to do to you? Now that I'm learning more about what you two did together, I'm becoming obsessed with your ass."

To punctuate his point, one hand slapped her ass cheek. The sting sent jolts of electricity straight to her clit. Blair gasped and then moaned. While Drake had never pulled her over his knees and spanked her like Grant had done many times, he had turned her on by slapping her ass whenever he'd taken her doggie style.

He hadn't hit her nearly as hard as Grant used to, but it'd still been hot and increased the strength of her orgasms. She'd always liked a bit of pain during fore-play and sex and now wished she hadn't held back that information from Drake, just taking what he'd given her and not asking for anything more.

As she set her hands on his shoulders to steady herself, Grant ran a hand through her drenched folds. "Yup, she liked that, brother. Oh, yeah, she definitely liked that." He held up his fingers, which were coated with her juices, for Drake to see how much that little slap turned her on. "I'm looking forward to reintro-ducing you to our play, Blair. I have a feeling Drake will love it as much as you and I do."

GOD, HE'D BEEN AN ASS, HIDING HIS DEEPER DESIRES from his wife. Drake was harder than ever, just thinking about pulling Blair over his lap and spanking her lush ass. He hadn't had a problem with a little slap and tickle during sex with her but had been too worried about her reactions to initiate anything more than that. She'd been so fragile and broken that first year after Grant's disappearance that Drake had handled her with kid gloves when it came to just about everything. After a while, it'd become a habit, he guessed. One he'd been afraid to break for fear of losing her. But that fear was gone now that Grant was back, and the three of them were on the same page.

After stripping his clothes off, Drake dropped to his knees behind Blair and nudged her inner thighs apart. "Spread them wide for me, baby."

As he kneaded her ass, he leaned back a little and got a great view of Grant's fingers penetrating Blair's pussy. Instead of jealousy raising its green head as he'd expected, Drake just got more turned on, and it felt like a final piece of a puzzle was being put into place. As much as he loved Blair, and she loved him, it seemed there had always been a tiny sense of something missing between them. Never in his wildest dreams had he thought it'd been Grant. Drake and his brother had never shared a woman in their lives, but he'd watched Grant have sex once before, with one of the few girls Grant had dated in high school before Blair. They'd been in the barn when an unsuspecting Drake had walked by. Moaning coming through a door that had been slightly ajar had easily caught his attention. Peeking in, he'd gotten his first live introduction to sex as Grant had fucked some girl whose name Drake couldn't remember. All he could recall was she'd been hot, willing, and loud, and she'd only been in Hazard for a few weeks that summer, visiting relatives. He and Grant had never seen her again after that.

Shifting his attention, he separated Blair's ass

cheeks and eyed the puckered rosette he was now dying to fuck. Unfortunately, he doubted that would happen tonight. It'd been a long time since she'd taken a cock there, and they would need to spend time prepping her so they wouldn't hurt her—he knew that much, at least. He'd let Grant take the lead on that, yielding to his experience since Drake had only been with one woman who'd been willing to try anal—once —and it'd been a long time ago. But that didn't mean he couldn't give Blair a taste of what would be coming soon.

Drake reached over to the second drawer in Blair's nightstand, where they kept a vibrator and some lube. He loved fucking her pussy with the vibe while sucking on her clit. Yeah, the sex he and Blair had might not be as kinky as she'd apparently had with Grant, but it definitely hadn't been hump-and-dump in the missionary-position-only kind of sex either. Although, with three young kids in the house, who often drained whatever energy both parents had left after working and doing chores all day, there had been more quickies lately instead of long, languid lovemaking sessions. Tonight would be different, though. If Drake had his way, the Hadley brothers would spend the entire night showing Blair how much they loved her.

Taking the lube, Drake squirted some down the crack of Blair's ass. She stiffened and gasped as if knowing his intentions without even asking before her muscles relaxed again. "Just my finger, baby," he assured her. "I want to tease you a bit before you and Grant start your feasts."

Her thighs quivered, and her ass clenched as Drake massaged the lube into her back hole. "Relax, Blair—I'll be gentle."

She moaned into Grant's mouth as she allowed her muscles to release their tension and thrust her ass toward Drake. Slowly and carefully, he pushed one fingertip inside her before pulling out and adding more lube. When he tried to ease in again, she threw her head back, panting and giving Grant access to her breasts, which he took full advantage of. Whatever he did to the taut peaks and her clit was enough to distract Blair, and suddenly Drake's finger breached the tight ring of her anus.

She was hot as hell as she squirmed between the two brothers. "Oh, Drake! Grant! Oh, shit! Don't stop! Please, don't . . ."

As Drake's finger fucked her ass, he brought his other hand up to her pussy. Grant was busy torturing her nipples and clit, so Drake slid two fingers into her tight, wet core. She rocked her hips back and forth, taking everything they gave her. Her moans, gasps for air, and murmurs of desperation filled the room. Drake's cock was dying to get inside her—anywhere inside her—but he wanted to watch her shatter for them first. From the looks and sound of things, it wouldn't take long.

Twisting his wrist, Drake's fingers searched for and

found her G-spot. He rubbed it and increased the pace and depth of his other finger in her ass. In front of her, Grant also magnified his ministrations. The quadruple assault quickly brought Blair to the edge. Her high-pitched keening told Drake she was ready to fly. "Come for us, baby."

Chapter 18

Blair needed no further encouragement or instructions. Grant's hand left her breast and moved to the back of her neck, pulling her mouth down onto his as her orgasm broke loose. She screamed into his mouth while her pussy and ass clamped down on Drake's fingers, almost crushing them. Blair shattering in the throes of passion was the most beautiful thing he'd ever seen. If it weren't for the kids, he would've planned on keeping her naked and sated for the foreseeable future.

The two men drew out her climax as long as possible until she finally sagged against Grant. Drake pulled his fingers from her body. "I'll be right back."

He stepped into their en suite bath and cleaned his hands with soap and water before returning to the bedroom. Grant had already adjusted himself, lying widthwise across the bed, his head about a foot and a half from the far edge. "Straddle my face, darlin'. Then lean forward so that Drake can fuck your sweet mouth."

The thought of his cock hitting the back of her throat had Drake nearly delirious with need. Gripping his shaft to keep from exploding, he circled to the other side of the bed while Blair climbed into position. "Remember, baby, if you come before I do, you'll get a spanking before Grant fucks you."

Between her spread thighs, Grant groaned. "Sure, make me suffer and wait to come. Although, I don't think I'll last more than a minute or two after getting inside her."

Drake grinned. Even though Grant had complained, Drake knew his brother would do everything he could to ensure Blair came first. As horny as he was, Drake had enough restraint to guarantee the same outcome—he hoped. They'd barely started this threesome thing, and it was already hotter than anything Drake had expected. Being naked and in the same room as Grant wasn't a big deal—they'd seen each other's junk plenty of times growing up. There was no incestuous attraction to make things uncomfortable and no embarrassment either. But watching Blair and Grant interact sexually was a huge turn-on, something Drake hadn't expected. Even though he'd agreed to try this ménage, he hadn't thought he'd be totally okay with seeing them pleasure each other. Not only was he okay with it, but now he couldn't wait to see more.

"What do I get if I make Drake come first?" she teased, her eyes dancing with delight and desire.

Standing before Blair, Drake replied, "We'll make you come until you beg us to stop. Now, spread your knees wider, and set that pussy on Grant's mouth."

The moment she did, Grant licked her slit, making her hips buck. "Delicious," was his muffled comment as Blair moaned and closed her eyes. A chuckle came from Grant. "Let the contest begin."

"Lean forward and take me, baby."

Blair's eyelids lifted again, and she bent at the waist. Her tongue came out and ran up the length of Drake's cock from root to tip. She gasped at something Grant did, and Drake took advantage of her open mouth. He thrust his hips forward, plunging his cock into her wet heat. One of the many things Grant had taught her during their time together had, apparently, been how to breathe properly while deep-throating. Drake was grateful for that fact since he'd enjoyed many nights with his cock down his wife's throat as she'd swallowed around him.

With her hands on his hips for balance, Blair squirmed and bobbed her head up and down as Drake used her mouth and Grant tortured her clit and pussy. She kept her warm gaze on Drake. Her eyes held nothing but love and passion—absolutely nothing for him to worry about. She was still his, but she was also Grant's. The brothers could give her everything she wanted and needed and more. And if something happened to Drake, Grant would take care of Blair and the kids, and vice versa. Grant could also watch and help his son grow up to be a good man—and not from a distance. After the stalker problem was over, the three adults would sit down and figure out all the issues they needed to work on for their ménage relationship to be successful. There undoubtedly would be some bumps in the road, but Drake was now certain this was meant to be. If Shane, Tucker, and Paige could make their threesome work, then so could the Hadleys. And if they had any questions or concerns, their friends were more than happy to give them seasoned advice.

Blair's tongue laved him as he pulled out of her mouth, then moved out of the way when he thrust in again, hitting the back of her throat. When she swallowed, he clenched his jaw and started doing multiplication tables in his head, refusing to go over the edge first. She was grinding her pussy onto Grant's mouth as the man devoured her, but she was avidly trying to get Drake to come before she did. Either way, she'd be rewarded—only one way would result in her ass being reddened first.

God, that thought almost made him come.

Nine times nine is eighty-one.

Ten times nine is ninety.

Eleven times nine is ninety-nine.

Twelve times nine is . . . is . . . ah, hell, who cares what it is?

When Blair's fingers tightened, digging into his hips, Drake knew she was close and thanked his lucky stars because he wouldn't last much longer. He smirked and reached down, pinching her nipples—all was fair in love and war, of course. Her eyes widened as she screamed around him, her orgasm disintegrating her. He held off his impending climax as long as possible so that he wouldn't choke her with his cum. After a few moments, her gaze returned to his, and she sucked hard on his cock. That was all he needed to let go. He stifled a roar as he spent himself, and Blair swallowed every drop.

She licked Drake clean as Grant eased out from underneath her and got to his feet. He quickly stripped, but Drake didn't pay him any attention until he heard Blair gasp. Grant froze as the two of them stared at his body. Healed scars and burn marks peppered his torso, shoulders, upper arms, legs, and groin. Sitting up with tears in her eyes, Blair reached out to touch a long scar underneath Grant's left nipple, but he grabbed her wrist with one hand and brushed away her tears with the fingers of his other hand. "Please don't cry for me, sweetheart. They've healed and no longer hurt. I've been seeing a shrink since my rescue and have learned to deal with them. While they're not pretty, they remind me that I went through Hell but survived it. We'll discuss them another time, but not now. There are far more enjoyable things I'd prefer to do with you right now."

Blair hesitated a moment before nodding. When Grant's gaze flittered to Drake's, the younger man swallowed the pity he felt, knowing his brother would hate it. With a nod, Drake pasted on a smile and tried to regain the mood they'd lost for a moment. "Grant's right, baby. We're not done with you yet, and I'm still dying to spank your ass."

After a moment's hesitation, probably to make sure they were all on the same page again, Grant retrieved a condom from his wallet, tossing both on the nightstand. There would come a day soon when prophylactics wouldn't be necessary, but Drake was happy his brother was taking the precaution until he'd gotten a clean bill of health.

Standing at the side of the bed, Grant flipped Blair onto her stomach, then pulled her hips up until she was on her knees. A giggle escaped her when Grant tapped her butt. "Keep your head down and this pretty ass in the air, sweetheart. Drake will give you ten slaps for coming first, and then I'll give you ten more. After your punishment is done, I'm going to fuck your pussy and pray I last long enough to make sure you come again. Okay."

"That's more than okay," she responded, getting into the proper position.

It looked like Blair was more than happy about getting a spanking. Whether that was because it really turned her on or she was looking for a way to get past the awkward moment they'd encountered over Grant's scars didn't really matter. Drake mentally shook his head, thinking of all the wasted opportunities he'd had to introduce more kink to their sex life over the years. Well, better late than never.

Grant took a step back and gestured to Blair's beautiful ass. "She's all yours, brother. Give her a good warm-up. Hard enough to sting but not bruise."

Drake was a little hesitant—he didn't want to hit Blair too hard and hurt her. Yeah, he'd slapped her ass while taking her from behind before, but those hadn't been real spankings—more like love taps, and he knew that's not what Grant was referring to.

As if sensing his brother's uncertainty, Grant moved forward and, without warning, swatted Blair's right ass cheek, then held his hand over the spot. The *crack* was loud in the bedroom, but Blair's startled gasp was followed by a sexy moan and wiggling of her hips that said she'd eagerly welcome another slap. When he pulled his hand away, her flesh was a pretty shade of pink.

"It sounds harder than it was," Grant said, stepping back. "She'll be drenched again by the time you reach ten. She'll be begging to be fucked before I reach twenty. Trust me."

Drake set a hand on Blair's lower back. "You'll tell me if it's too much, baby?"

Glancing over her shoulder at him, she smiled. "I trust you both not to harm me, but I'll let you know if I can't take anymore." She winked and wiggled her ass again. "Now give it your best shot, stud."

He couldn't help the grin that spread across his face. God, he loved her. "Brat."

Rearing back, he swung his hand toward her buttocks, aiming for the left cheek. The crack wasn't as loud as when Grant had hit her, but Blair still moaned.

"Harder," Grant instructed. "And not in the same spots—overlapping is fine, but spread them out. You can hit her upper thighs and sit spots too."

Drake aimed the next slap under the curve of her right ass cheek, a little harder than the first. Blair yelped, then begged, "More!"

Grinning, Drake was more than happy to oblige her. With each slap, he grew harder, even though he'd just come a few minutes ago. By the time he reached ten, Blair's ass and upper thighs were pink. After admiring his handiwork for a moment, he eyed his brother, who nodded. "Very nice. That pink is a nice shade on her, but wait till you see it when it's red." Grant ran his hand over her tender skin. "How're you doing, sweetheart? Good to continue?"

"I'm good . . . please don't stop." She was a little breathless, and her body had a fine sheen of perspiration. If he put his hand between her legs, he knew she'd be drenched for him.

"That's our girl. Drake, go around and watch her face." When Drake's eyes narrowed, Grant continued. "I'm going to be hitting her harder than you did, and I want you to observe her reactions. Let me know if you don't think she can handle it anymore. But remember, I'm also going to be reading her body language. She'll be crying before I'm done, but it's not a bad thing."

When Grant's first strike landed, Drake jumped, his eyes widening. Grant could almost hear what his brother was thinking. That'd been a lot harder than his demonstration spank at the beginning, but even if Drake didn't think Blair could handle it, Grant knew better. While neither he nor Blair had ever been into dominance and submission or sadism and masochism, they had enjoyed bondage and spanking, along with some other light forms of play that were probably common in BDSM circles. Grant wouldn't give Blair more than what she could take from him. And if she told him to stop, he would.

By the third slap, he knew she was crying. But that didn't stop her from asking him for more. Drake kept his gaze on her face but clearly didn't see a reason to halt her fun-ishment. That was good—it meant he was reading her facial expressions and body language correctly. As he peppered her ass, Grant's cock demanded he stop playing around and fuck her. His little head would get its wish soon, but not before

Grant delivered the grand finale. After six spanks, he massaged both globes of her ass. "I won't pause for the last four—they'll be hard and fast. Then I'm going to take you the same way. All right?"

"Y-yes! Please!"

Grant eyed Drake, silently asking if he agreed she was still good to go. When his brother nodded, Grant landed the last four smacks in rapid succession—the first two on her sit spots and the final ones right across the middle of her ass.

"Ahhhhh, shit," she cried out. "Hurry, Grant! Fuck me, please!"

"As much as I'm tempted to take you from behind, I want to watch your face this time," he said almost reverently. He grasped her ankles, flipped her onto her back, and then reached for the condom on the night-stand. While her cheeks and jaw were stained from her tears, her eyes pleaded with him. She was holding on by a thread, and it wouldn't take long for her to come.

After he sheathed himself, Grant climbed onto the bed and settled between her thighs. Her pussy wept with need, glistening in the light from the lamp on the nightstand. His cock was super-sensitive, desperate to get inside her for the first time in eight years. When he glanced at Drake, a flash of uncertainty appeared on the younger man's face. Not wanting his brother to feel like a third wheel, Grant said, "Kiss her and play with her nipples. I meant it when I said I won't last, and I want her to come again before I do."

He knew his words had the desired effect on Drake because the apprehension had disappeared from his face. Drake smiled and nodded. Leaning down, he captured Blair's mouth as his hands found her breasts, pinching and pulling on the taut peaks. Grant watched them, enjoying how quickly Drake got her writhing again. Unable to wait any longer, Grant lined his cock up with Blair's waiting entrance, then thrust inside her. He was far from being gentle and hoped she wouldn't mind because his restraint was gone.

Her hips bucked, taking him deeper, and Grant slammed his eyes shut as her warmth surrounded him. Despite an apparent healthy sex life and having given birth to three children, Blair's cunt was still tight and fit him like a glove that was a size too small. Grant groaned. He was balls deep inside her but remained still. It would only take three or four thrusts before he came. While Drake was getting her worked up, Grant needed things to speed along. Reaching between his and Blair's bodies, he fingered her clit. The combined assault proved too much for her overly responsive body. When he felt the starting quivers of her impending orgasm ripple around him, Grant pulled almost all the way out and plunged in again. Blair ripped her mouth from Drake's. "Oh, God! I'm coming!"

Two more passes along her rippling vaginal walls, and Grant exploded, coming harder than he ever had in his life. His body sagged against hers as Drake left them alone momentarily and stepped into the bathroom. Grant stared down at the woman he loved. She was still gasping for air but reached up and caressed his sweat-soaked face. "I love you."

Grant's heart soared at her declaration. He finally felt he'd come home. Before tonight, he'd been a visitor in his childhood house, but now, he was back where he belonged. "I never stopped loving you, sweetheart. And I never will."

When Drake returned with a damp washcloth, Blair's gaze shifted to him. "And I love you too. Thank you both for not making me choose."

After handing Grant the washcloth, Drake leaned down and brushed his lips over Blair's. "I love you too, baby, and I always will."

Once Grant had disposed of the condom and cleaned Blair up a bit, Drake turned her until her head rested on a pillow in the middle of the king-sized bed. Grant didn't miss how he'd left plenty of room for both of them to lay down on either side of her. Grant climbed into bed and stretched out beside Blair, putting his arm across her body, just below her breasts. Drake did the same on the other side, with his arm across her waist. Within minutes, all three of them were sound asleep.

Chapter 19

Three days later . . .

W hen Blair hesitated to take Grant's hand so he could help her from the middle seat of her SUV, he smiled at her. "Having second thoughts? We can go back home if you want."

"No!" the three kids shouted in unison, having obviously overheard Grant from the backseat.

You promised, Mom," Trevor added. He was the one who would be the most disappointed if they didn't head into the fairgrounds. Her oldest was signed up to ride in the mutton-busting competition. He'd be going up against other seven-year-olds to see who could stay on the back of a sheep the longest. She didn't want everyone to remain behind locked doors, even though there was an implied threat against them. If they gave in to their fears, the bad guy won. That wasn't to say they wouldn't be taking precautions today—Vic, Manny, Bruce, and Liam had parked their two SUVs next to theirs, one to the right of Blair's and the other directly behind it. The men had followed them there and would walk around with them, keeping them all safe. As nervous as Blair was, she didn't want to give in to her fears—not when the kids had been looking forward to today for months.

Putting on her best smile, she took Grant's hand. "Nope, we're staying. I was just trying to remember if I'd packed the sunscreen."

The expression he gave her said he knew she'd told a white lie, but he completely understood why. He leaned in as she got to her feet and whispered, "We'll keep you and them safe—I promise."

She gave him a chaste peck on the cheek—which was now soft and smooth after he'd shaved this morning—since they'd agreed to keep their newly established threesome to themselves for now. "I know you will."

"I wanna hold your hand, Uncle Grant," Regan announced as she jumped down from the backseat. "And I wanna go to the petting zoo."

"Holding hands and the petting zoo, you've got it, sweetie. Let's go."

As he took the little girl's hand, Blair felt a sense of rightness come over her. Grant belonged with them, and she would do everything in her power to ensure he stayed with them at the end of this stalker mess. However, they still had to face the inevitable shitstorm they'd stir up when the townspeople found out Grant was home for good and would share Blair with Drake. While many people would be supportive, just as they were accepting of the Wilsons' ménage marriage, there were plenty who would be against it and damn them to hell. More than once, Paige had suffered having drops of holy water splashed on her by some of the pious church ladies of the town. At least, neither Blair nor Drake was a churchgoer, so they wouldn't have Pastor Harrington staring at them from the pulpit on Sundays.

Trying to forget the four armed men who surrounded them were there to protect her family, Blair took Drake's and Michael's hands as they all followed Grant, Regan, and Trevor, who told everyone his strategy for remaining on the sheep for the required six seconds. Of course, he'd be wearing a helmet for when he eventually fell off. Next year would be the last he'd be eligible to enter due to the five-to-eight-age range for the event. Blair hoped he didn't want to continue riding after that since he'd move up to the bull calf riding competitions, but she'd support him if he did. She'd just cringe when he couldn't see her. So far, Regan was only interested in riding horses and not the kind that bucked. She was supposed to start taking lessons later in the month at a friend's horse farm, but if the stalker issue wasn't resolved by then, Blair would postpone it.

It was a beautiful day out, and even though it was a Friday, the parking lot was already packed. The amateur events would run today and tomorrow morning, and even more people would attend the professional events scheduled for tomorrow evening and Sunday.

"Blair!"

She searched the crowd and spotted Paige waving at her. The other woman pushed her youngest daughter in a stroller as she joined them. Letting Drake take Michael, Blair stopped, peeked at the sleeping child, and then hugged her friend. "Where's Ari?"

They fell into step behind the others, with two of the bodyguards coming up in the rear.

"She already dragged Seth to the petting zoo while Shane and Tuck went to check out the bull stock." Years ago, Tucker could've gone pro in bull riding but had decided against it since there was no guarantee he could make a well-paying career out of it. However, he still participated in a few local amateur rodeos each year, especially the one in Hazard, and was usually the man to beat. He'd be riding in the preliminaries this afternoon and likely the finals tomorrow. The Hadleys would be cheering him on from the stands along with the rest of his family and friends.

"We're headed to the petting zoo too. I thought you

were working the admission ticket booth again this year."

"Tomorrow and for a few hours on Sunday. Three days in a row is too much. Shane and Tuck would've been fine with Ashley and Ari all day, but Nicole had enough volunteers to take slots, so I've got today off, thank God. Who knew standing in one spot all day could be so tiring?"

Blair completely understood. For two years, before Regan was born, she'd helped out for a full day at the rodeo while Drake had minded Trevor, then they'd switched, and he'd worked wherever the organizers needed him the next day. As Drake's business grew over the next few years, he set up a tent with the other vendors and sold many of his smaller pieces while growing a customer base for made-to-order furniture. This year was the first he didn't have a vendor booth since he'd started—he rarely had time for non-custom work anymore since he was taking orders for six months from now. She knew he missed doing the "just for fun" pieces and wondered if he could make some again with Grant helping out in the workshop. He wasn't in there often, spending most of his time looking for the stalker, but he'd talked about the fun he'd had, tinkering in the shop with his brother. In fact, the two men had been laughing about old times when they'd returned to the house for dinner last night after spending about two hours together in the workshop.

Despite the stress she knew Grant was under, he

seemed happier over the last few days. Of course, their threesome and sexual aerobics probably had something to do with that.

"So, you don't have to go into details," Paige said in a low voice while leaning toward Blair, "but how are things between the three of you? Any progress?"

Blair felt her cheeks heat up, and when she didn't answer, Paige turned to face her fully and chuckled. "Never mind, your blush says it all. Good for you. Didn't I tell you it was delicious having two men lovin' on you at the same time?"

She wasn't sure if Grant had overheard Paige, but Blair's face reddened even more when he glanced back at her and winked. Damn, it was going to be hard hiding her feelings for him in public now.

Somehow, they'd made it all the way to the ticket booth before someone recognized Grant behind his dark sunglasses and cowboy hat. It wasn't long before they were surrounded by locals who'd known him most of his life. The four bodyguards stayed close to Blair, Paige, and the children while Drake and Grant fended off the curious masses, giving vague answers to questions thrown at them. It wasn't until Regan and Michael began to whine about wanting to go to the petting zoo that the two men finally got the crowd to disperse and let the family enjoy their day out.

Once the small group got moving again, they passed by some of the vendor booths, and Paige nudged Blair and then gestured to their left. "Check out Bridget."

The obnoxious woman wore a pure-white linen dress that accentuated her perfect size-four figure and red heels as she showed a large painting to an older couple. While everyone else at the dusty rodeo was dressed in denim jeans or shorts, boots, and T-shirts or western shirts, Bridget looked ready to take Soho in New York City by storm. How her makeup wasn't melting off her face was beyond Blair.

Bridget glanced in their direction, and her eyes went wide when she spotted Grant. She excused herself and ran over to him, throwing her arms around him and shocking the hell out of him and those around him. "Grant! Oh my God, it's true! You're alive! Let me look at you." Without releasing him, she leaned back and ogled him. "You're as handsome as ever and so muscular too. I'll never understand how Blair left you to return to this godforsaken town. We should go out some—"

The woman was practically purring and drooling as she ran her hands over his broad shoulders and chest. Blair was about to step in, but Grant grasped Bridget's upper arms and moved her back a few steps away from him. "Blair didn't leave me, Bridget. As far as she and everyone else knew, I was dead. And for someone who hates this town as much as you do, I'm surprised to see you still live here after all these years. You should check out Washington, D.C.—I'm sure you'd fit in perfectly with the sharks there. As for going out with you, I've got better things to do. Now, if you'll excuse us, we have a petting zoo to get to. Forgive me for not saying it was a pleasure to see you again."

Paige and Blair did their best not to burst out laughing at the stunned and indignant look on Bridget's face when Grant picked up Regan and started their group moving again. The other woman glared at them before turning on her heel, almost falling on the uneven ground, and returning to her booth.

Behind Blair, Manny snorted and chuckled. "God, I love small-town drama."

Blair had no idea what Bridget thought she'd accomplish by her little display. Grant hadn't liked the woman back in high school—she'd hit on him relentlessly, even after he'd started dating Blair—and it was obvious his opinion of her had never changed.

After Manny's statement, the two women couldn't hide their laughter. Blair realized it was the first time since she'd received the photo of Grant on her phone that she'd laughed so hard her stomach hurt. It felt good, and suddenly, she pushed the anxiety of the stalker to the back of her mind and looked forward to a fun day with her family and friends.

Chapter 20

It'd been a long day for both the adults and the kids. Between all the fun things to see and do, watching the amateur rounds of rodeo events, and everyone wanting to talk to Grant, the Hadley family was exhausted. While Blair held Regan in her arms and Drake carried Michael, Grant gave Trevor a piggyback ride as they trudged toward the parking lot. Grant wanted nothing more than to get home and put his feet up for a while, although he'd had a fun time with Blair, Drake, and the kids—better than he'd expected. They'd stayed long enough to see Tucker ride a bull named Stone Cold for eight seconds to make it to tomorrow's final round. He'd won the amateur event the last two years and was going for a three-peat. Of all the bad-ass and risky things Grant had done in his youth and the CIA, getting on the back of a pissed-off, 1700-pound animal had never been something he'd been willing to try. Not in this lifetime—probably not in the next one, either.

Surrounded by four of Grant's "friends," with their concealed weapons, they weeded their way through the rows of vehicles in the packed parking lot. Vic and Grant led the way, not stopping for anyone else who wanted just a moment of time from the man who'd come back from the dead. Grant did his best not to sound rude as he brushed people off. He understood he would be Hazard's side-show freak for a few weeks until everything settled down and someone or something new sparked the small town's interest. For now, he just had to put up with it.

The last few days, sleeping in the master bedroom with Blair between him and Drake, had settled him in a way he hadn't expected. While the horrified look in Blair's eyes when she'd first seen his scars had rattled him, he'd done his best not to let her know it'd upset him. The next morning, while the kids played in the backyard after breakfast, he'd given Drake and Blair the much watered-down version of how he'd gotten all the scars. His captors' favorite way to torture him was holding a lit cigarette to his skin. There were times he could still smell the vile odor of burning flesh. But he'd been truthful when he'd told them his shrink, Dr. Trudy Dunbar, in Tampa, had helped him deal with the aftermath of his abuse. She was friends with Sawyer and his teammates and was also on the government's approved list for counseling special-ops veterans who had loads of classified data in their heads. While he couldn't tell her a lot of the details of where he'd been held captive and why, she hadn't needed them to treat him.

The one thing Trudy hadn't been able to help him escape, though, were his nightmares. But for the past few nights, lying next to Blair, he'd slept soundly, without waking up in a cold sweat and a scream on his lips. He never woke up swinging but, instead, frozen in fear. At first, he'd been ashamed about that. He'd definitely fought the North Korean soldiers any time he was able to, but his nightmares seemed to have the opposite effect on him. Trudy had explained that sometimes a person's mind dealt with the horrors it'd gone through differently after the real threat was gone. Grant was under no illusion his nightmares wouldn't return—and he, Blair, and Drake would deal with that when it happened—but for now, he was grateful they were being held at bay.

Once Blair's SUV was in view, for some reason, the hair on the back of Grant's neck raised, and a warning tingle shot down his spine. His head swiveled around as his eyes darted in every direction. Beside him, the special-ops agent was doing the same, but he'd been doing that all day. Grant wasn't sure if Vic sensed something awry now or if Grant's instincts were off. Something didn't feel right, but he didn't spot anything or anyone out of place. They only had to pass one more row to get to the SUV, and Grant couldn't see anyone near it.

"Uncle Grant, can I get down?" Trevor asked.

"Sure, sport." After making sure no vehicles were coming toward them from either direction, he bent his knees a little and let go of the boy's thighs as the hands around his neck released him. Trevor was about to run toward the SUV when something caught Grant's eyes, and he grabbed his son by the shoulder, stopping his forward momentum.

Trevor looked up at him in confusion. "What's wrong?"

Two steps ahead of Grant, Vic stopped short and scanned the area, his hand at his lower back where his weapon was hidden. He glanced over his shoulder at Grant. "What is it?"

"Look next to the driver's door of Blair's SUV."

A muttered curse told Grant the other man had quickly zeroed in on the problem. Drake stopped next to his brother. "What's wrong?"

"Someone's been underneath the driver's side." Grant pointed to the disturbed dirt and gravel sweeping away from the SUV. Someone had slid out from underneath the vehicle.

Dropping to his knees, Vic cautiously bent down and peered under the chassis. A low "damn" reached Grant's ears, and he knew his fear had been confirmed. Vic got back to his feet, and his gaze zipped to Manny's. "Get them in the other vehicles and get out of here. Check 'em first, though—it's a pipe."

Without hesitation, the other hired men grabbed Trevor's, Drake's, and Blair's upper arms and quickly steered them toward one of the other SUVs. The operatives' gazes were alert, taking in their surroundings. Drake and Blair looked at Grant with a combination of shock and alarm in their eyes. Not wanting to scare the kids, Grant made an explosion gesture with his hands and made sure the adults understood him. "We'll call the sheriff and have this taken care of. I'll see you back at the house later. Do everything Manny, Bruce, and Liam tell you to do. It'll be all right."

Before opening the doors, Manny crouched down and inspected the undercarriage of the SUV he'd driven into the lot earlier. Declaring it safe, he opened the rear door for Blair. "Get in."

Wide-eyed, she turned to Drake but also glanced back at Grant. "We need the car seats."

Grant shook his head. The last thing they needed to do was stand out in the open, arguing about car seats. "Don't worry about the seats. The guys know how to drive in the worst conditions—y'all will be safe. Just buckle the kids in." Any other time, Grant would've given in to the need for the seats, but there was no way of knowing if the pipe bomb was rigged to the engine or one of the doors being opened or any other action for that matter. His family had to get out of there—they were in more danger of the bomb than a car accident at this moment, and the other two operatives would be following Manny back to the house to guarantee their safety.

As the adults bundled the kids into the back of the SUV, they put Trevor between Blair and Drake and sat Michael and Regan on their parents' laps. Meanwhile, Manny had whipped out his phone and called the other operatives monitoring the family from a discreet distance throughout the day. They would be waiting at the exit to the parking lot to escort the others home.

Once he was sure his family was safely on their way out of there, Grant pulled out his own phone and hit the speed dial for Lane. "We've got a problem in the parking lot," he said without preamble when the other man answered. "How soon can you get a bomb squad here? And how fast can you evacuate the area?"

"Fuck me. Where are you exactly?"

"North end, fourth row out, about seven vehicles from the end." He scanned the lot. There were dozens of people milling about, walking to or from their trucks or cars, and laughing without a care in the world. Little did they know there was a pipe bomb under Blair's SUV.

"We're on our way."

Grant saw mounted and foot patrol officers closing in on their location in under a minute. The police and sheriff's deputies immediately started shifting the public away from where Grant and Vic stood. Laughter turned to confusion and even a few arguments, as no one could understand why they were prevented from returning to their vehicles. But they weren't Grant's problem right now.

Even though he trusted Vic's knowledge and assessment, Grant squatted down and peered under the driver's door. Sure enough, someone had attached a pipe bomb to the undercarriage. Going around to the passenger side, Grant took a look at the device from that angle too. Thankfully, there didn't appear to be a timer or wires leading to any of the doors, which meant it was probably rigged to the ignition and would've gone off when the engine was started.

As he got to his feet and joined Vic at the front of the vehicle, Chief Hughes, Lane, and one of the deputies hurried over. The latter was introduced as a member of the sheriff's bomb squad, Deputy Hudson Stokes. After Grant gave them a quick rundown of the situation, Stokes dropped down and wriggled under the SUV to better understand what he was dealing with. "Huh. Hey, did either of you touch this?"

Grant squatted down and peered under the chassis at the man. "You're kidding, right?"

"I know—stupid question, but I had to ask. It's not live." He used a small mirror at the end of an expanded handle to examine the device from every angle.

"What?"

"It's not connected to anything." He pulled on the edges of the silver strips holding the metal canister against the undercarriage. "It's just a timer Duct-taped to an empty canister. The top is missing, and there's nothing in it."

Stokes crawled from under the vehicle and handed the dud device to Grant. Sure enough, the canister was useless—thank God. Grant muttered a curse before turning to the other men. "It's another warning that this bastard can get me or my family at any time and any place. He's fucking toying with me, and I'm sick of it."

"I don't blame you," Chief Hughes responded after telling Tad Winslow to have the officers and deputies return to their assigned posts for the event and allow people back into the parking lot. "But it doesn't get us any closer to figuring out who he is and what his end game is."

The man was right, but it just made Grant's anger boil even more. He ran through possible options in his head. If he left town, trying to lure the stalker away, there was no guarantee he'd follow. If Grant stayed and waited him out, they could be the bastard's puppets for weeks or months. If they tried to send Blair and the kids away and reduce the number of targets, how could they be certain the stalker wouldn't follow them instead of staying to mess with Grant? Three options and none of them were viable, in his opinion.

Lane took a step forward, his arms over his chest. "Two more days and ninety percent of the tourists and rodeo people will be gone by Monday morning. The fewer people around, the harder it will be for this guy to blend in. If we step up our search, maybe it'll force him out into the open, but we have to wait until the rodeo clears out."

Grant knew the lawman was right, although none of them were happy about it right now. Grant had learned to be patient as an undercover operative, but that was a quality he no longer possessed—at least when it came to his family's safety. But now, he'd have to figure out how to control his impatience. Two more days, then he'd hunt the bastard down. And if the stalker were lucky, Lane or one of the other cops would find him first.

Chapter 21

Three nights later, Drake and Grant had offered to treat Blair and the kids to dinner at Bar None, accompanied by Vic and Manny, after she'd forgotten to plug in the slow cooker with a pot roast inside. She felt like such an idiot but blamed it on the stress she'd been under. While things were fine between her, Drake, and Grant, she couldn't stop worrying about the stalker, even though they were heavily guarded. Liam and Bruce were in the parking lot with a pizza, watching over the vehicles—they weren't taking any chances this time—while the other guards were watching the Hadleys' house and property.

The restaurant was pretty busy for a Monday night —mostly locals, though. A majority of the rodeo people and tourists had pulled out of town throughout the day, but a few remained. Blair hadn't missed how

Grant, Manny, and Vic had situated themselves at the round, eight-seat table so they could see the entire room and everyone coming and going through the front and back exits. If anyone suspicious approached their table, the two guards could quickly get up and put themselves between the others and any danger. Blair doubted anyone would be stupid enough to attack them in a crowded restaurant, but then again, what did she know about stalkers? About as much as she knew about spies.

Music from the jukebox was playing a mix of new and old country and classic rock, as it usually did on most nights. On the dance floor, a few couples were two-stepping to Tim McGraw's latest song. Several people had waved to the Hadleys when they'd first walked in, but aside from their waitress, no one had approached their table . . . until now.

Blair sighed. She really wasn't in the mood to deal with Bridget, but the bitch definitely had something on her mind. Dressed in a red, knee-length skirt, white blouse, and white heels, she looked like she'd just come from her new gallery. From the glare she gave Grant, she was still pissed about his brush-off the other day. Bridget's attention diverted to Blair when she stopped between Drake and Trevor. "So, word is you've decided to follow your perverted friends and screw two men—"

She never had a chance to finish. Drake and Grant got to their feet to interrupt her, but Manny, the good-looking Hispanic bodyguard, stepped over to Bridget and spoke first. "Excuse me." He smiled brilliantly and held out his hand. "I'm Manny Cortez, and you are?"

Bridget's jaw dropped as she took in his handsome features and well-toned body, but then she gave him a seductive grin and shook his hand. "I'm Bridget Kline. It's nice to meet you."

"I don't know if you remember, but I was there the other day when you threw your arms around Grant to welcome him home." Bridget's smile faltered as she tried to figure out where he was going with this. Blair was just as intrigued, especially after his comment about small-town drama that'd made her and Paige laugh. "I remember thinking I should hit on you. I mean, you're not bad looking—a little skinny for my taste, but I could look past that for a few hours if you know what I mean." The woman's eyes widened at the insinuation. "But then you walked over here and opened your mouth, and I realized just how unpretty you really are. Number one—you weren't invited to join us. Number two—no one asked for or wants your opinion. Number three—what these people and everyone else do in the privacy of their own homes is none of your business. Number four—young children who don't need to hear about your distaste for their parents are present. Number five—if you don't turn yourself around and take a hike, you'll regret it. And, no, I'd never hit a woman, but there are other ways to get my point across."

For the first time in his speech, Manny's mouth

turned into a frown—he'd been grinning the entire time as if putting the woman in her place was an everyday entertaining occurrence. When he crossed his arms over his massive chest, Blair realized the entire restaurant had gone quiet, except for the jukebox, and everyone was watching Bridget get her ass handed to her. "Now, I suggest you leave before the owner of this fine establishment throws you out herself."

Bridget had rage in her eyes when she looked over her shoulder to see Lou trying her best not to laugh out loud and cheer Manny on. When she saw the bitch glaring at her, Lou's expression became stern. "The man's right, Bridget. Get out before I throw you out. I've warned you before about harassing my customers."

Spinning around to Manny again, red-faced and looking for a way to salvage her pride, Bridget opened her mouth, but the man cut her off again. "I suggest you think really hard before saying whatever's on the tip of your tongue because, truthfully, you haven't seen me pissed off yet. Now, if you'll excuse me, our waitress is bringing our dinner."

Without another word or a backward glance, Manny took his seat again and made a display of shaking out his napkin and putting it on his lap. Behind Drake, Bridget's mouth opened and closed several times as she glanced around, looking for support. She had none. Pivoting on her ridiculously high heels, she stormed across the dance floor toward the front door. Someone from another table started clapping, then another person joined in, followed by a third until almost the entire restaurant was laughing at the woman's expense and applauding.

Once the bitch was gone, Lou came over, slapped Manny's shoulder, and laughed. "Your drinks and dinner are on the house tonight, Manny. That's the best entertainment we've had here for a while now."

The man looked up and winked at her. "I'm available whenever you need me, Lou, but I get paid double for Friday and Saturday nights."

Everyone at the table chuckled while the rest of the place returned to their own meals and conversation. After the waitress distributed their dinners and took another drink order, Manny focused on Blair. "Don't ever let anyone make you feel ashamed for loving two men—and yes, Vic and I figured that out long before whatever-her-name-is said anything. In my eyes, putting up with these two makes you stronger than most women. Hell, I can't even get one woman to put up with me, and it would be even harder if I added my brother to the mix. Although that would never happen since we don't get along, but I digress. While I've never been in a ménage relationship, I do know a few people who are, and I don't see anything wrong with it. Do what you think and feel is right, and to hell with everyone else."

"That's a bad word," Trevor piped up for the first time since Bridget had walked over. "The h-word."

Manny grinned at the boy and ruffled his hair.

"You're right, partner. It is a bad word, and I apologize for using it in front of you and your mom. I'll tell you what—to make up for it, I'll treat you to a game of pinball when you've finished your dinner if it's okay with your parents."

Trevor's eyes lit up. "Can I, Mom?"

Blair couldn't say no. "If you eat everything on your plate, you can play one game with Manny." Her gaze shifted back to the man, and she smiled. "Thank you. For everything."

Drake held out his hand to the bodyguard. "Same here. You're welcome in our home any day, my friend."

Taking his soda glass, Grant clinked Manny's and silently toasted him. Blair glanced around the room. No one was pointing at them or seemed to be even talking about them, although a few were still laughing and gesturing toward Manny and then at the door Bridget had walked of. She didn't know how the bitch had figured out about the ménage relationship, but it didn't really matter. Maybe this three-way relationship wouldn't be a major issue for most townspeople. Either way, Blair found she didn't care. All that mattered was that she, Drake, Grant, and the children were happy and safe. The first thing was taken care of, so all she had to worry about now was the second one.

Chapter 22

The next day, Grant returned to the house after two hours of driving around, searching for someone out of place, now that the last of the rodeo crowd had finally cleared out. Unfortunately, he'd had no better luck finding the bastard who'd been fucking with him and his family.

Parking the SUV in the driveway, he got out as Vic approached the vehicle. "I take it from your expression nothing has changed."

"Nope," he responded, slamming the door harder than necessary. "This fucker is on my last nerve." Glancing to the side of the house, he noticed the trailer Drake used to transport finished furniture to his clients was missing. "Where's Drake?"

"One of his clients called and asked if he could deliver her desk today instead of tomorrow. He couldn't get a hold of one of his movers, so I sent Bruce with him—killed two birds with one stone. They were going to some address in Willsboro, so it'll be a while before they get back." He glanced at his watch. "They only left about fifteen minutes ago."

Willsboro was way on the other side of the county, about a forty-minute drive if you were doing the speed limit, which Drake would be with the heavy trailer attached to his Chevy Silverado. Drake had several men he used on an as-needed basis to help him move the bigger pieces of furniture, but he usually had them scheduled in advance. Even though Bruce was more than capable of helping Drake carry the desk into the woman's house, Grant wished he'd gone with Drake instead of the bodyguard, leaving him here to help watch over Blair and the kids.

As if he knew what Grant was thinking, Vic snorted. "We've got the house well-guarded, and Bruce is carrying, so your brother is safe too. He didn't want to call you away from your search and was going to tell the woman he couldn't get it there until tomorrow, but when I suggested Bruce go with him, Drake agreed."

Taking a deep breath, Grant let it out. "Sorry, I know you guys can handle anything that comes your way, but I wish I could take my family away from here and go somewhere safe, but that's impractical at the very least."

"Yup. You could be hiding for months, and that's not living."

"I know . . . still doesn't make me feel any better about not packing the family up and disappearing."

Liam exited the house through the front door with Roscoe on his heels. The dog ran to the closest tree to do his business as the bodyguard strode toward Grant and Vic. "Apparently, it's nap time, and Michael's not happy about it. He's screaming his head off, so Roscoe and I came out here before our ears started bleeding."

The other two men chuckled. That was one of the things Grant was trying to get used to. The kids weren't always happy and sweet, and he was still trying to figure out where he stood when it came to disciplining them or comforting them when they were hurting. It was the only time he really felt like a third wheel since he'd started sharing Blair with Drake. They'd tried to reassure him it would take time for the children to realize and accept his new role in their lives. They still called him "Uncle Grant," for now, and the adults had agreed to keep it that way until after the threat to the family was gone and Grant's "friends" were no longer needed. Before they went public about their ménage relationship, they'd sit down and explain things the best they could to the kids and hope they understood.

Deciding to try to give Blair a hand with the four-year-old, Grant started toward the front door of the house, but his cell phone ringing had him stopping short and pulling it out of his back pocket. Glancing at the screen, he saw it was Lane Myers and answered the call. "Hey, Lane, what's—"

"Drake's missing, and his bodyguard's been shot."

Shock then panic surged through him. "What! Where—"

"Saw Mill Road, just west of the old Coleman farm. The truck and trailer are in a ditch. Got an ambulance en route for the guard—he's alive but unconscious."

"I'm on my way." Without disconnecting the call—Lane did it for him—Grant gave Vic a quick recap while hurrying to his SUV.

The former SEAL skirted the front of the vehicle and jumped into the passenger side after ordering Liam to call the other guards in from their hiding spots and to lock Blair and the kids in the house. "I'll call as soon as I have an update. If anyone tries to gain entry to the house, shoot first and ask questions later," he instructed through the open window as Grant threw the vehicle into gear and spun out on the driveway.

Through the rearview mirror, Grant watched Liam run into the house. He was torn between staying here to watch over Blair and the kids and going after his brother, but Drake was the one in immediate danger at the moment. With six well-trained bodyguards protecting the rest of his family, Grant knew what he needed to do, and that was to find Drake.

With his phone now reconnected to the vehicle's Bluetooth feature, Grant called Lane back. "Can you send any marked cars to the house? Even though there are six guards with Blair and the kids now, I want whomever this bastard is to know he's not getting anywhere near them if this is some kind of distraction."

"I'll see what I can do."

"Thanks. We'll be there in a minute." The Coleman farm, which had stood empty ever since its owner had died without any heirs when Grant had been a teenager, was about three miles from the Hadleys' home. During his daily drive-arounds, he'd noticed there was construction equipment there. Apparently, some developer had recently bought the property and was preparing the land to build several new houses. For now, though, that stretch of road was basically empty and a good place for an ambush. Drake had obviously been taking Saw Mill Road out to County Road 26, which would've taken him straight to Willsboro.

After ending the call with Lane, Grant dialed Blair. She probably already knew something was wrong and would be freaking out more if he didn't let her know what was going on—not that he had much information himself.

"Grant! What happened? Liam—"

"I don't have all the details, sweetheart, but Drake's truck was found on the side of the road, and he's missing."

"What? Oh my God! What happened?"

He refused to tell her that Bruce had been shot—it would just terrify her even more. "I don't know yet, but we'll find him, I swear. This bastard wants me, and he'll use Drake to get me to come to him. Trust me, Drake will be okay and be home with you soon." He prayed like hell he was telling her the truth because the alternative was too unbearable to voice.

"Now, you listen to me, Grant Hadley." There was a hint of anger below her distress. "You *both* better be home soon. I love you both, and you're not putting me through that again. Do you hear me? Not after I just got you back. I trust you to find Drake and bring him home *with* you."

God, he loved this woman. "I'll do everything I can, sweetheart." Up ahead, two SUVs came into view with their overhead lights flashing. "I gotta go. Do everything Manny, Liam, and the others tell you to do. Lane's sending a patrol car or two there as backup."

"Okay. I love you, Grant."

He could tell she was holding back tears. "I love you too, baby. I'll call you as soon as I can."

Pulling in behind the second of two police SUVs, Grant could now see Drake's trailer was mostly on the shoulder of the road, with the Silverado grill-first into a large culvert. An ambulance and a paramedic fly-car were parked past the disabled vehicle, and the first responders were loading a stretcher with Bruce on it into the back of the rig. From the distance between them and the fact that there was an oxygen mask over the man's face, Grant couldn't tell if Bruce had regained consciousness.

Before Grant was able to throw the vehicle into park, Vic had the passenger door open and jumped out, running toward the ambulance and his wounded man. Grant was about to climb out of the driver's seat when his phone rang again. The screen said the number was blocked, and he knew this was the bastard calling to let him know he had his brother.

Grant turned off the engine so the Bluetooth feature would disconnect before he answered the call and put the phone to his ear. He didn't bother with pleasantries. "Who is this?"

He was surprised when a male voice responded in Korean. "I am the man who will kill your brother if you don't come to me—alone."

"Where?" he responded in the same foreign language. He'd save the questions of who? and why? for later when he had his gun against the son-of-a-bitch's skull.

When the man rattled off some numbers, it took a moment for Grant to realize they were coordinates for longitude and latitude. After grabbing a pen from the center console and still speaking in Korean, Grant told the kidnapper to repeat the location as he wrote it down on a scrap of paper. After getting the coordinates again, Grant demanded to talk to his brother—he wanted proof of life.

He was starting to think the man wouldn't comply, but then Drake's voice came through the phone. "Grant! Don't do what he says! I—"

When Drake was abruptly cut off, Grant looked at the phone's screen to see the call had been disconnected. He sent up a prayer, hoping that meant Drake hadn't been permanently silenced. He'd never forgive himself if his brother were killed because of Grant's past.

Bringing up a map app on his phone, he plugged in the numbers. The map quickly zoomed in on an unincorporated area about twenty minutes away from Hazard Falls. The place was surrounded by woods, and, as far as Grant knew, the few buildings still there had been abandoned long ago after several consecutive years of severe flooding of a nearby river had run the residents off. There had been no businesses there, just a few family homes.

Lane knocked on the driver's window, and Grant rolled it down, not knowing how long the man had been standing there. "The bastard just called to say he's got Drake. The coordinates he gave me are for Chesterfield. I take it that's still a dead zone." He winced, realizing what he'd just alluded to.

"Yup, it is. Did he give you any clue as to who he is and what he wants?"

"No, but he's definitely not from around here. He spoke in Korean."

"Korean? So, it *does* have to do with your CIA days."

"I guess, but I couldn't care less about that right now. I'm supposed to go alone, but I'm not stupid enough to do that." He saw Vic running back to the truck before asking Lane, "You coming? I don't want a whole brigade rushing in there, but between you and Vic, my back will be covered, and we'll take this jackass down."

"You got it. I don't even have backup at the moment. There's a domestic on the other side of town with shots fired. The chief, Tad, and everyone else are headed that way. I called the sheriff's department and had them send someone to your house. I'll call them back and have them dispatch a car to cover this scene too. Give me two minutes, and I'll follow you."

"Make it one," he responded with a nod as Vic jumped back into the passenger seat. Turning to the guard, Grant gave him a quick situation report, then asked, "How's Bruce?"

"I think it looks worse than it is," Vic said as the ambulance pulled away from the scene, its lights and sirens announcing the urgency of their call. "He's moaning, so hopefully, that means he's coming around. The medics said he hit his head on the passenger door frame, which is the reason they think he's unconscious and not from the bullet. Despite everything, they said his vitals were good. They'll know more after they get him to the ER and have a CT-scan done."

A horn beeping had Grant looking through the windshield to see Lane signaling for Grant to pull out in front of him. Once they were on their way toward Chesterfield, Vic called Manny and updated him on Bruce's status and what was happening with Drake.

Grant was still worried this was a ruse to draw attention away from where Blair and the kids were being guarded, so he said no when Vic asked if he wanted Manny to catch up to them. Grant, Vic, and Lane all had specialized training. As long as Drake's kidnapper was working alone— Grant was almost positive he was —then three against one was all they needed.

He prayed he was right.

Chapter 23

The dampness of the rotted wood floor Drake was sitting on seeped through his jeans, making him shiver despite the temperature hovering around seventy degrees. Apparently, their stalker had been hiding out in the abandoned buildings in Chesterfield while they'd been searching for him. The unincorporated area was far enough out of Hazard Falls, and many people had forgotten about its existence, so it made sense that no one had thought to check the place out. There were no signs of human life remaining in the dilapidated house, but it looked like small creatures had been using it for shelter. Droppings from mice, birds, and raccoons were scattered about. All the windows had been knocked out, and what had once been floral wallpaper in the living room was peeling and curling away from the decaying drywall. A few broken pieces of furniture remained but were covered in mold and mildew.

The only things that were new and out of place in the house were the Asian man's sleeping bag, camping gear, and weapons. On his hip was a 9mm pistol, while resting on an old end table was the sniper rifle he'd used to shoot Drake's bodyguard. God, he hoped Bruce was alive.

Drake had been a little surprised when his client, a forty-year-old woman who was a bestselling author, had asked if he could bring her custom-made desk to her today instead of tomorrow. She'd explained that she was having unexpected company coming tomorrow and wanted it in place to show it off. She'd even said she would understand if that wasn't possible, and if it wasn't, they'd have to move the delivery to the following day. Drake hadn't thought it would be a big deal to bring it early, but then none of his per-diem guys could help him with the last-minute change. When Vic had suggested taking Bruce along for both protection and lifting help, both men had easily agreed. When he wasn't doing private security work, Bruce helped out his brother-in-law with his moving busi-ness, so he'd been more than willing to give Drake a hand. Talk about bad timing.

While Drake had been doing the speed limit on Saw Mill Road, a van had approached them from behind, going about forty miles per hour faster than that. At first, Bruce had been wary and unbuckled his seatbelt and pulled out his weapon, just in case, but the vehicle had passed them and kept going. There wasn't much along that stretch of roadway, and people rarely did the speed limit unless they had a reason to, like hauling a trailer. But when they'd rounded a slight curve, they came upon the same van pulled over to the side of the road. Drake remembered thinking it served the guy right to break down seconds before his windshield cracked and Bruce had grunted in pain. A second gunshot had taken out the right front tire, causing Drake to lose control as the truck veered off the road into a ditch. Because Drake still had his seatbelt on, he didn't get thrown around the interior of the cab as harshly as Bruce had been. The guard had been knocked unconscious. Before Drake could assess whether the man was still alive and breathing, the driver's door had been flung open and he'd been dragged out of the front seat at gunpoint by a man who was far stronger than he looked. A punch to his temple had stunned him long enough that he hadn't been able to resist being handcuffed. After being unceremoniously thrown into the rear compartment of the van, he'd ended up in this abandoned house.

While the man had spoken to Drake in moderately accented English, he'd used a foreign language while talking to Grant on the phone. If Drake had to guess, it was Korean. Aside from giving some simple directions to his captive—"sit down and shut up"—the man had refused to talk to him further or answer any questions.

Now, all Drake could do was look for a way to assist in his own rescue and wait for Grant to bring the cavalry —he was certain his brother wouldn't come alone, despite the kidnapper's order. Drake knew there was only so much he could do with his wrists handcuffed behind his back, but his legs were still free. Hopefully, there'd be a moment when he could kick the guy off balance or something.

The quiet surroundings were driving Drake nuts, increasing his anxiety. All he heard were birds chirping and unseen animals scurrying around outside the opened windows, while his unnamed captor moved on silent feet as he kept checking all points of entry, waiting for Grant to show his face.

Deciding to try to get some information out of the guy again, Drake asked, "Can you at least tell me why you're after my brother?"

Moments passed, and Drake didn't think he was going to get an answer, not that he'd expected one, but then the man turned toward him and glared. "As you disgusting Americans say, an eye for an eye. Your brother was a spy who was looking for ways to take my government down. It's not enough that you have to destroy your own country, but when you come after mine—we will do whatever it takes to stop you."

Still confused, Drake shook his head. "I don't understand why you said, 'an eye for an eye.' What did Grant do to you?"

"It is because of him that my own brother is dead.

And now, before I kill him, I will kill his only sibling, so he knows what it feels like."

Well, that sucks.

Glancing around again, Drake tried to find a way to prevent Blair from losing not one but both men she loved. Maybe if he could keep the guy talking and distracted, it would help Grant stage an attack. He remembered something Lane had told him one time —a lot of criminals were sociopaths and those that were liked to brag that they were smarter than everyone else. The trick was to get them talking. Once you did, they began to fill in the silence on their own. "Why are you blaming Grant for your brother's death? He was in a mountainside prison from what he told me."

His captor checked three windows before responding this time. "My brother was one of the guards your government killed on that mountainside. Your military, or whoever it was, illegally crossed into North Korea and slaughtered everyone to break your brother out of prison."

"And your government had illegally arrested him, tortured him, and kept him in a cage when he wasn't in a hole in the ground," Drake barked, his anger over-taking him. "So, you don't get any sympathy from me!"

The man strode over and towered over him, his eyes flaring in ire. "It is not sympathy I want. It is revenge. And I will have it. I was the only person to survive that . . . that massacre. When I returned from reporting to my superiors, I found the bodies of my men . . . of my brother."

If the bastard hadn't held Grant prisoner for years, torturing him, and then going after Blair and the children, Drake might have felt sorry for him. *Might* being the operative word. "How did you know who Grant was and how did you find him?"

He sneered. "The internet is a wonderful thing, and so is facial recognition technology. We took several photos of our prisoners over the years. Like your United States, my government also employs computer specialists—hackers, as you call them. It took a few months, but, eventually, your brother was given a Florida driver's license with his picture on it in a different name than what your CIA had given him. You can thank your wife for helping us connect the dots from there. You stupid Americans put your entire lives on social media, giving anyone the information needed to find you. Her memorial to him on Facebook several years ago was quite touching."

Shit. He was definitely not going to tell Blair that— if he got out of there alive, that is. When she and Grant had been living in D.C., Grant had told them not to post any pictures of him on the internet because of his alleged position with the Secret Service. But after his "death," Blair had written a beautiful tribute to Grant and posted it along with the last picture she had of them together. It was the one and only time she'd put a picture of him on her profile. For months after that, she hadn't even been on Facebook. It wasn't until after Trevor was born that she'd gotten active on it again, showing off photos of her little boy.

"So, how does it feel to be married to your brother's whore, hmm?"

Drake saw red and yanked on his restraints. "Fuck you! Don't you dare use that word for her." He'd give anything to be able to put his hands around the bastard's neck and strangle him.

The man snorted and then went back to checking the windows and doors. Over the roar of his anger, Drake heard an approaching vehicle.

What the fuck? Grant's pulling right up to the front door?

It didn't make sense to him—Grant had to know he'd be ambushed. Unless he brought backup. That had to be it.

So, I have to be ready to help them in any way I can.

While his captor's attention was on whatever was happening outside, Drake rolled onto his side and tried to pull himself up onto his knees. The other man heard him, pivoted, and aimed his pistol at Drake's head. "Lay on your stomach, or I'll shoot you right now."

Reluctantly, Drake complied.

Chapter 24

The dirt road leading into what little was left of Chesterfield was full of potholes, causing Grant to drive slowly. They'd stopped about a mile ago and left Lane's patrol vehicle, and he'd jumped into the back of the SUV. When they were a half mile from where they'd be in full view of anyone in the ramshackle homes, Grant tapped the brakes to allow Vic and Lane to exit from the front and rear passenger doors. The two men disappeared into the trees, where they'd double-time it toward Drake and the kidnapper's location, taking extra precautions not to trip any boobytraps along the way. According to Lane, there were only three buildings still standing—barely—so it shouldn't take long to zero in on the right one.

On the drive over, Vic had been pissed at himself for only sending one man with Drake. Grant kind of knew how the guy felt. They'd been so focused on keeping Blair and the kids safe that they hadn't really considered Drake would be a main target. Grant was certain that's what their stalker had wanted them to believe. And now, Drake was in a position he'd never been trained to deal with. No matter what happened in the next few minutes, Grant was determined to make sure Blair got both her men back. But if it came down to only one of them returning to her, it would be Drake. Grant's brother had helped her through losing a man she loved the first time it'd happened. He could do it again.

As the woods opened into a large clearing, it was obvious which of the three remaining buildings they would be in. Two of them were missing half their walls, and a dark blue van was parked next to the third one. Grant brought the SUV to a stop a fair distance away from the dilapidated house, eying his surroundings and giving Lane and Vic a chance to get into position. He rolled down all four windows and listened for a moment. Other than the sounds of nature, nothing else caught his attention.

In the center console, his phone vibrated. Lane had sent a text message, confirming he was south of the clearing and didn't see any signs of an ambush or boobytraps. They'd created a group chat for all three of them to communicate since the lawman was the only person with a handheld radio. A few moments later, Vic's text said he was also in place.

Leaving the SUV where it was, with the engine running in case they had to make a fast escape, Grant climbed out of the driver's seat and didn't bother closing the door. As he walked slowly toward the house, he held his gun in his right hand. No sense in hiding it—the stalker/kidnapper surely wouldn't have expected him to come unarmed. Lane had also given Grant a .38 caliber pistol, which was now strapped to his right ankle. The officer figured Grant would probably have to toss the 9mm before getting close enough to his target, so he'd need the backup piece before Lane would.

Grant couldn't see inside the building since it was much brighter outside.

"I'm here, you bastard," he yelled in Korean. "Show yourself, or are you too much of a coward?"

Calling any man a coward was sure to piss him off, but saying it to a North Korean was the equivalent of cutting off his manhood.

From inside the house came a string of foreign curses and insults, most of them aimed at Drake and Grant's mother. They were followed by an order for Grant to drop his weapon and come into the house with his hands up, or Drake would get a bullet in his head. It looked like Lane had been correct with his prediction—not that Grant had expected otherwise.

After setting his gun on the ground, he slowly approached what had once been the front door to the house. Again, he was giving Lane and Vic a chance to move in closer from the south and north, respectively. Stopping in the doorway, he waited for his eyes to adjust to the darker interior. There was no way this bastard was going to shoot him right away. He hadn't been fucking with them all this time to just end it now without any drama or fanfare. He'd figured he had all the time in the world, out there with no one else around to interrupt whatever he had planned.

"In!" the man barked, this time in English. "Inside! Now!"

When Grant complied, he finally connected the horrors of his past with that of his present. Yung Nam-Kyu had been a lieutenant at the prison camp. His younger brother, Yung Min-ki, had been one of the guards—one of the now-dead guards that Carter, Sawyer, and the rest of the rescue team had killed. So, this was all about revenge, and Drake had been the target all along. Blair and the kids had been ruses to draw the attention away from the real objective. An eye for an eye. A brother for a brother.

Yung stood above Drake, who was face down on the rotted wooden floor, aiming his pistol at his captive's head. Drake's hands were cuffed at the wrist behind him.

"You okay?" Grant asked his brother. He doubted Drake would believe he'd come without backup, but hopefully, the other man wouldn't think it.

Drake shrugged his shoulders the best he could in that position. "Right as rain. Although I could do without the handcuffs, damp floor, the big-assed spider that just crawled up to the ceiling, and the gun pointed at my head, but, hey, beggars can't be choosers, right?"

"Shut up!" The North Korean ordered Drake before sneering at Grant. "So, we meet again, Evan Walker. Or should I say, Grant Hadley?" He reached behind his back, produced another set of handcuffs, and tossed them to the floor in front of Grant. "Put them on."

When he just glared at him, Yung gestured with the gun. "Do it! In the back."

In no rush, Grant set one metal cuff around his left wrist with a click, and then putting his hands behind him, he fumbled a moment until he closed the second one around his right wrist. He may have lost the use of his hands, but he'd been trained to fight without them. With any luck, he wouldn't need to go that route with Vic and Lane still outside and unknown to Yung.

Grant turned slightly and wiggled his fingers to show the other man his hands were indeed restrained. "This is a little unfair, isn't it? I mean, your brother and the other guards had a fighting chance. This is cheating, in my opinion."

He stepped further into the room to his right, forcing Yung to pivot as well, away from the window closest to him. Lane would be coming from that direction. Vic's advancement would be concealed by the kitchen's windowless north wall in the other room, which Grant had spotted upon entering.

"I do not care for your opinion—it means nothing to me. Revenge is all that matters."

Grant didn't doubt it, but he had to keep the bastard talking until the cavalry arrived. Silently, he urged Lane and Vic to hurry the fuck up. "How did you find me?"

Yung snorted as if Grant was an imbecile. "I am not repeating myself. Your brother can fill you in when you both reach Hell."

He pointed the gun at Drake's head again, forcing Grant to make a move. He rushed forward, hoping the muzzle would switch to the greater threat. Yung's eyes widened, and his hand came flying up. A gunshot filled the air, and Grant cringed briefly before realizing he hadn't been hit. An expression of shock covered the North Korean's face, and blood bloomed on his shirt and drizzled from his mouth. He crashed to his knees and fell to the side. Lane appeared in the window, ready to fire another shot if necessary.

Vic ran into the living room from the kitchen, his gun at the ready. After quickly taking in the scene, he kicked the gun out of Yung's hand and then bent down to check for a pulse. Grant doubted there was one, and a moment later, Vic confirmed it. "Right in the heart. Nice shot, Lane."

Rolling onto his side and struggling to stand, Drake was white as a sheet. "I agree, but next time, could you not wait until the last possible second?"

Grant smirked. "Hopefully, there won't be a next

time." He stepped over to the window, putting his back to it and sticking his hands out a little toward Lane. "Now, get me out of these fucking things while Drake fills me in with whatever that asshole told him."

And while he got his heart rate under control. Holy shit, that'd been close. Grant would forever be in Lane's debt, as well as that of all the bodyguards'. Because of them, he had his family alive and well—all of them.

Twenty minutes later, the abandoned town of Chesterfield was bustling with activity. The domestic on the other side of Hazard Falls had ended peacefully with no injuries and one person under arrest. When Lane had called in the shooting, the local law enforcement responded in force. There would be hours of interviews, paperwork, and scene processing. Immediately after Grant and Drake had been uncuffed, they'd called Blair to tell her they were both fine and unharmed. When she'd started crying in relief, Grant wished they could run to be with her, but they'd needed to remain at the scene. Manny had assured him the guards would take care of her and the kids until the brothers could return home.

After Drake called his client to let her know he'd been delayed and would have to reschedule her delivery, Grant took a moment to ensure his brother was okay. The color had returned to Drake's face, but he still appeared shaken about the whole incident. Grant also had something else on his mind. "You know, there's always a chance my past can become a problem for us again."

Drake's eyes narrowed at him. "So?" He paused, glancing down at the ground and then up again. "Look, I know this could've ended a lot uglier than it did, but if your past is the only thing making you consider leaving town again, don't be an ass. If something else happens down the road, we'll protect Blair and the kids —together. But, Grant, what happens if your past comes back to Hazard, and you're not here to help me protect them? The last thing I want is for you to leave. It'll break Blair's and the kids' hearts . . . it'll break mine too. You're my brother, and the only place I want my brother is by my side, loving our woman and raising our kids. Understand?"

Grant snorted, then smiled. "When the hell did you get to be so smart?"

Chapter 25

Under the warm shower spray, Blair let the last of the fear and tension drain from her body, along with the tears she'd held back for hours. After being checked out by the paramedics and giving their statements to Chief Hughes and the county sheriff, Drake, Grant, and Vic had finally been cleared to go home. The sheriff's department would investigate the incident instead of the Hazard Falls PD since Lane had been involved. Grant had told a worried Blair it was standard procedure, and none of them, especially Lane, were in any trouble because it'd been a justified shooting.

Blair had never been more relieved in her life than she was when the two men she loved walked in through the front door. Shaking, she'd thrown herself into Drake's arms, then pulled at Grant's hand until he was behind her, sandwiching her between them. Within moments, their warmth seeped into her ice-cold body, leaving her shivering for a whole new reason. Unfortunately, there'd been children and company in the room.

Liam had called from the hospital and reported that Bruce was conscious and alert. The bullet had gone through his shoulder and out the back, not hitting anything vital. The doctors expected him to make a full recovery. When Drake crashed the truck, his passenger had been knocked out. Thankfully, Drake had kept the North Korean from putting another bullet into Bruce.

Because no one had been in the mood to cook, Vic and Manny had volunteered to drive over to Bar None and pick up dinner for everyone. In the meantime, Drake and Grant had taken showers and changed into clean clothes. While the other guards had packed up and headed home since they were no longer needed, Vic and Manny had decided to stick around for a few days to ensure the threat was definitely over.

While the kids had been watching TV in the family room, the adults had gathered in the kitchen, where Drake, Grant, and Vic had filled Manny and Blair in on the details of the kidnapping and rescue. While Blair wasn't sure they'd told her everything, from what they *had* told her, she didn't really want to know all the gory details. Their stalker/kidnapper was dead, and her men and children were safe and unharmed—that's all she cared about.

A few hours later, just after 8:30, the two body-guards had bid them goodnight, and Drake and Grant had told Blair to relax while they read a few bedtime stories and tucked the children into bed. It took every-thing in her not to follow them upstairs to the kids' rooms. She'd been afraid to let them out of her sight, worried she'd been dreaming and that she'd lost both of them. Despite her fears, she'd turned and strode into the master bedroom, where she'd stripped and stepped into the shower. It was there she'd finally broken down.

Blair didn't know how long she stood under the pelting water before the shower curtain slid open, and Grant stepped in behind her, gloriously naked, despite the scars and old burn marks on his skin. She was getting used to seeing them, but she still had to force herself not to show him any pity. He wouldn't accept that emotion from her when it came to the reminders of the abuse he'd suffered. Besides, they were a testa-ment to his strength and determination to return to her.

When she tried to turn around to face him, he stopped her by putting a hand on her shoulder. Without saying a word, he picked up her shampoo bottle, squirted some in his hands, and began working it into her locks. His fingers massaged her scalp, and she almost purred because of how good it felt. Grab-bing the handheld showerhead, he gently rinsed her hair, then repeated the process with her conditioner. Once her hair had been taken care of, Grant retrieved the pink loofah sponge hanging from the water temperature handle and added a dollop of lavender-scented body soap to it. Starting at her neck, he washed every inch of her body, all the way down to her toes, spending extra time on her breasts, pussy, and ass. By the time he rinsed the suds off her, she was so aroused she was ready to beg him to take her right then and there.

Before she could say anything, though, he turned off the water and opened the curtain. Standing there was Drake, holding a big fluffy towel. Grant took Blair's hand and steadied her as she stepped out of the tub. As Drake wrapped her in the towel, then got another one and began to dry her hair, Grant left the room with his unsatisfied and very hard erection. By the time her husband had dried her from head to toe, Blair was even more aroused. Neither man had said a word to her other than giving her directions to move or stand a certain way, so they could pamper her.

After she was towel-dried, Drake took a palmful of Blair's favorite body lotion and slathered it on her, even dropping to his knees to get her legs and feet. Once he was done, he looked up at her. "Spread your legs, baby. I want a quick taste before Grant says he's ready for us."

"Ready for us? What's he doing?" she asked while still complying with his order.

With a smile, he ignored her questions and leaned

forward. When his tongue swiped across her clit, before delving lower, Blair almost lost her balance. She put her hand on the counter for support as Drake licked her pussy, moaning as he did so. His hands went around to cup her ass, and Blair lifted her right foot and set it on his shoulder, opening herself up more for him as he continued to eat her. It didn't take long for the stirrings of an orgasm began to grip her under his ministrations. Her breathing increased, as well as her heart rate.

"Please, Drake. Oh, God! Please!"

When two of his fingers pushed into her hot, wet core, her climax tore through her. She cried out as she coated his tongue with her juices. Her legs shook, and her eyes slammed shut at the onslaught of sensations.

Finally, Drake released her, setting her foot back onto the floor. When Blair opened her eyes, she wasn't surprised to see Grant standing in the doorway, watching them. He was still naked and hard.

Holding out his hand, Grant beckoned her to join him. "Come here, sweetheart. We're far from done with you yet." The look of desire on his face told her she would enjoy whatever they had planned.

As Drake began to strip out of his clothes, Blair walked toward Grant on trembling legs and let him take her hand. He led her into the bedroom, where dozens of lit votive candles in little glass jars were spread around the room. They provided the only light in the now-darkened room. Drake had done the same thing for her on their last anniversary and had apparently pulled them out of the box she'd stored them in.

Pulling her into his arms, Grant kissed her passionately. She squirmed against his body, heightening her arousal. When Drake joined them, Grant released her and instructed his brother to lie on the bed. Once he was in position, Grant lifted Blair and set her so she was straddling Drake's hips. "Get in her, brother, while I prep her ass. We're going to take you at the same time, sweetheart."

Blair shivered in anticipation. Every time they'd had sex, one of her men had been fingering her ass, stretching her so she could one day have them inside her ass and pussy at the same time. Apparently, today was that day.

Lifting up on her knees, she allowed Drake to line his dick up with her slit, then lowered herself down onto him. He groaned loudly as he thrust his pelvis upward. She was still slick from the orgasm he'd given her, and soon he was in her as far as he could go. He held her hips a moment. "Stay still, baby. Otherwise, I'll be coming before Grant gets inside you." She could see on his face the restraint he possessed, but it would clearly be hard for him to wait more than a few minutes before he snapped.

Reaching up, Drake played with her nipples, pulling and rolling them. Behind her, Grant pushed gently on her back, angling her closer to Drake's chest. Then she felt the cool lube dripping into the crack of her ass. While the cock inside her twitched in impatience, one finger, then two pushed into her ass, scissoring open to stretch her. Apparently, Grant didn't have much patience at the moment either because it wasn't long before his fingers were replaced with the head of his cock.

"Finger her clit and kiss her, Drake," his brother said. "Distract her for me."

Blair knew it would burn and hurt a little until her body adjusted to the initial invasion. Still, she also knew from experience that once Grant was balls deep inside her, that pain would morph into something incredibly pleasurable.

Getting his hand between them, Drake rubbed her clit with his fingers, then used his other hand to clasp her neck and pull her mouth down to his. His tongue plunged inside her mouth, claiming her, as his fingers drove her desire higher and higher. Behind her, Grant began to penetrate her. At first, it was uncomfortable, but Blair tried not to tense and allowed Drake to distract her as Grant had requested. Grant didn't rush, allowing her body to ease into accommodating him. He pushed in slowly, then retreated again. Each time, he tunneled further inside until he breached her sphincter and slid all the way in.

Blair lifted her mouth from Drake's, panting and

struggling against the numerous sensations bombarding her. "Oh—oh God! Please! Fuck me . . . both of you! I need you to fuck me!"

"Who are we to deny such a request?" Drake asked before he thrust his hips upward.

"Damn, she's so fucking tight," Grant said through gritted teeth. "I'll pull out as you push in. We should be able to establish a comfortable rhythm."

As Grant dragged his cock almost completely out of her ass, lighting up all the nerves inside her, Drake moaned. "Holy fuck! I can feel him, baby. While it should weird me out, it doesn't, knowing your body is separating us."

"Fuck! What he said! You feel incredible, sweetheart. So much tighter than I remember because he's inside you too."

Alternating between thrusting and retreating, her men fucked Blair senseless. It wasn't long before her body was on the edge, ready to explode again.

"Oh, fuck, Blair! I can't stop!"

Grant plowed into her and froze as he spent himself deep inside her. That triggered her own release. Burying her face in the mattress beside Drake's head, she screamed as her pussy and ass clenched around the two cocks. A few more thrusts and Drake followed them into the abyss.

As they all collapsed into a sweaty and breathless heap, Blair sent up a silent prayer of thanks to the powers that be for keeping her men safe and sending them back to her. No matter what their future held, they'd face it together as a threesome. To hell with anyone who had a problem with it because there was no way she would choose one brother over the other. They were the two pieces of her soul that completed her, and she was never letting either one of them go.

Epilogue

Under a beautiful blue sky, Grant watched as Michael shared a piece of his tangerine with Trident Security operative Marco DeAngelis's little two-and-a-half-year-old girl, Mara. At the same time, her father frowned at them from a few feet away. Grant chuckled because he knew if it were some snot-nosed kid flirting with Regan, no matter how young, he and Drake would be having hissy-fits too. God help them both when she was old enough to date. On the other side of the yard, between two buildings at the TS compound in Tampa, Trevor, Regan, and Parker and Shelby's two seven-year-old boys were feeding fish food to the koi in the pond. The Hadley clan had taken the hour-and-twenty-minute ride from their hotel near Disney World to visit Grant's former boss and coworkers, the private security teams who'd helped rescue him, and their spouses and kids. Carter and Jordyn had even managed to fly in from wherever they'd been to visit as well.

It'd been six weeks since Yung Nam-Kyu had been killed, and the Hadley family's lives had been righted again. It hadn't taken long for the brothers, Lane, and Vic to be cleared in the man's death, so the following week, Grant had flown to Florida with Vic and Manny for a quick round-trip. The two men had volunteered to help him pack up his apartment and drive the rented truck back to Kansas. One of the last things Grant had taken care of before leaving the Sunshine State was to transfer the back pay he'd received from the government, covering his six years in captivity, which he'd left collecting interest in a bank, to another bank in Kansas. After returning to Hazard Falls, he'd sent his former foreman's architect boyfriend, Linc Perry, the original floor plans of the house the Hadley brothers had grown up in to design a new addition. Drake and Blair agreed to make a new, larger bedroom suite to accommodate the three of them. Blair had been thrilled with the plans for a whirlpool tub and walk-in shower, both of which could fit the threesome comfortably. She'd also been thrilled when she'd seen the cozy reading room he'd asked to be put in for her, where she would have a quiet place to work on her book translations.

Once he finished the addition, Grant would turn their current master bedroom into an office for himself and the company he was starting—Cornerstone

Construction. While he loved tinkering in Drake's workshop, Grant knew he wasn't as talented as his brother when it came to creating fine furniture, but the construction business was something he could do well and enjoy.

Rhys Buchanan and Linc strode over to where Grant stood as Drake left him to grab a soda since he'd be the one driving back to Orlando in a little bit. Rhys slapped Grant on the back. "I sure do miss you, man. You were one of my best workers, but I'm really glad you got your family back."

When Grant had spoken to Parker and Rhys about leaving New Horizons and Tampa, he hadn't been able to clue them into his past with the CIA and his imprisonment. So, instead, he'd lied a bit and said the reason he'd been separated from his brother and his wife was because of a misunderstanding that had led to a falling out between them. After reconnecting with them, they'd reconciled and were now involved in a ménage relationship. Since both men were Doms and belonged to the discreet BDSM club located on the other side of the compound, neither had blinked an eye about the two brothers sharing a wife. In fact, there was another threesome at the barbecue—Ian Sawyer's cousin, Mitch, with his boyfriend, Tyler, and girlfriend, Tori. Apparently, theirs was a full ménage relationship—the men were in love with each other as well as their woman—and they were in the process of planning their wedding. Grant had hoped Remi and Grayson

Mann could stop by with their fiancée, Abigail, since Shelby had mentioned they'd been invited. Blair would've loved to have met another woman who was in a loving relationship with two brothers. Unfortunately, the record producers and Abigail were currently in England for some big music event.

Grant lifted his beer bottle and lightly tapped Rhys's in a toast. "Thanks. You were a great boss, but I'm definitely back where I belong. If you two are ever in Kansas, give us a ring. You're more than welcome to come for a visit."

Smiling, Linc responded, "We might just take you up on that someday. I'd love to see how the new addition turns out. I think this is the first time I didn't have an in-person walk-through of an existing building that I worked on. I expect to get before and after pictures emailed to me for my portfolio and website."

"You've got it. And thanks again for the design—we really love it. Finding a local architect I can refer people to is on my to-do list."

In fact, that list was quite long, but Grant didn't mind it at all. Between him, Drake, and Blair, the lines of communication were open more than they'd ever been. Grant had been taking the time to get to know his brother and the woman they loved all over again, and Drake and Blair were exploring the fantasies they'd kept hidden from each other for so long. Somehow, without much effort, both men had managed to spend private time alone with Blair—sometimes involving sex, while other times they just talked or went shopping or some other mundane activity. But that didn't mean when Drake and Grant took her together, it wasn't as sexy and intoxicating as hell.

They were also all getting used to consulting two other people when it came to making decisions that affected the family, but there had been very few disagreements so far. What had surprised Grant the most was how easily the kids had accepted their new "Pa," as they now called him. Trevor had been excited to tell Arianna that he now had two dads, just like she and Ashley did. The adults had agreed he was still too young to understand the dynamics behind his birth, but they planned to consult with a child psychologist as to when and how they should explain it to him. Honestly, it didn't make a difference to Grant since he loved all three children as if he'd been their sole biological father.

A smile crossed his face. He was a father in every sense of the word. That was something he never thought would happen during the past eight years. Each morning, as his family surrounded him at the breakfast table, he thanked God things had turned out the way they had. While a part of him would always regret what he'd put Blair through following his alleged death, when he looked at Michael and Regan, he knew he wouldn't have changed a thing. This was how their family was meant to be.

"Pa! Look!" Regan cried out with a giggle as Parker's

huge bullmastiff, Spanky, and Sawyer's lab/pit mix, Beau, sat in front of her, somewhat patiently waiting for the treats she'd been allowed to give them. They were both well trained, but their butts were wiggling in anticipation.

Grant stepped over to her as each dog gently took a bone-shaped biscuit from her outstretched hands. As the dogs hurried away with their prizes, Grant picked Regan up in his arms, and she smiled at him and kissed him on the cheek. As it always did now, his heart swelled with love for the little girl he called his daughter. Drake had asked a lawyer friend of his to draw up official documents that gave Grant guardianship over all three children if anything happened to him or Blair. While Grant couldn't legally adopt them or marry Blair, they'd ensured everyone would be well cared for if tragedy struck.

"Having fun, pipsqueak?" he asked her.

"Uh-huh. Spanky's even funnier than Goofy."

Grant chuckled. "He sure is."

"But I miss Roscoe."

"I'm sure he misses you too, but Uncle Shane promised they'd take good care of him while we're gone."

She seemed to ponder that for a moment. "Can we call Uncle Shane so that I can talk to Roscoe on the phone? I don't want him to forget us."

Grant squeezed her. "You're unforgettable,

pipsqueak, but yeah, we can call them when we get back to the hotel later, okay?"

"Okay."

Drake returned, carrying Michael, whose eyes were almost completely shut in exhaustion, while Blair steered Trevor in their direction. It looked like it was time to say goodbye to the people who'd come to mean a lot to Grant over the past year and a half. He'd be forever grateful to each and every one of them.

Going up on her tippy-toes, Blair kissed Grant and then Drake, clearly at ease with public displays of affection toward both men now. The first few times the three of them had gone out together, Blair had obviously been shy and worried about reactions from the residents of Hazard Falls. But thanks to Paige, Shane, and Tucker, it wasn't anything most of them hadn't seen before. Yeah, there were comments and looks of disdain from the bigots and bible-thumpers in town, but for the most part, the new threesome had been accepted.

Glancing down to Blair's left hand, Grant once again admired the wedding ring he'd presented to her before they'd left for Orlando. He and Drake had returned to the jeweler, who'd designed the one Drake had given her on their second anniversary, to replace the simple band they'd purchased when their marriage had only been one of convenience. The jeweler had created a new ring that complimented the other one perfectly, and now Blair wore both her men's symbols of love.

"Time to get going?" Blair asked as she eyed her children.

Drake nodded. "Yup. Michael will sleep the entire ride back, I'm sure."

It'd been a long and wonderful day, but Grant was looking forward to spending the evening alone with just his family. Then, after the kids were tucked into their beds in the two-bedroom suite Grant had splurged on, he and Drake would take their woman and, once again, prove to her how much they loved her. It was something Grant planned on doing for the rest of his life.

Want to read more about T. Carter, Ian Sawyer, and the rest of the Trident Security gang? Start with *Leather & Lace: Trident Security Book 1.*

Other Books by Samantha Cole

***Denotes titles/series that are only available on select digital sites. Paperbacks and audiobooks are available on most book sites.

THE TRIDENT SECURITY SERIES

Leather & Lace

His Angel

Waiting For Him

Not Negotiable: A Novella

Topping The Alpha

Watching From the Shadows

Whiskey Tribute: A Novella

Tickle His Fancy

No Way in Hell: A Steel Corp/Trident Security Crossover (co-authored with J.B. Havens)

Absolving His Sins

Option Number Three: A Novella

Salvaging His Soul

Trident Security Field Manual

Torn In Half: A Novella

Burning For Him

***HEELS, RHYMES, & NURSERY CRIMES SERIES**
(WITH 13 OTHER AUTHORS)
Jack Be Nimble: A Trident Security-Related Short Story

***THE DEIMOS SERIES**
Handling Haven: Special Forces: Operation Alpha
Cheating the Devil: Special Forces: Operation Alpha

THE TRIDENT SECURITY OMEGA TEAM SERIES
Mountain of Evil
A Dead Man's Pulse
Forty Days & One Knight

THE DOMS OF THE COVENANT SERIES
Double Down & Dirty
Entertaining Distraction
Knot a Chance
Finding His Forever
Reclaiming His Soulmate

THE BLACKHAWK SECURITY SERIES
Tuff Enough
Blood Bound

MASTER KEY SERIES
Master Key Resort
Master Cordell

HAZARD FALLS SERIES

Don't Fight It

Don't Shoot the Messenger

THE MALONE BROTHERS SERIES

Her Secret

Her Sleuth

LARGO RIDGE SERIES

Cold Feet

***ANTELOPE ROCK SERIES

(CO-AUTHORED WITH J.B. HAVENS)

Wannabe in Wyoming

Wistful in Wyoming

AWARD-WINNING STANDALONE BOOKS

Where the Broken Bloom

Scattered Moments in Time: A Collection of Short Stories & More

***THE BID ON LOVE SERIES

(WITH 7 OTHER AUTHORS!)

Going, Going, Gone: Book 2

***THE COLLECTIVE: SEASON TWO

(WITH 7 OTHER AUTHORS!)

Angst: Book 7

About Samantha Cole

USA Today Bestselling Author and Award-Winning Author Samantha Cole is a retired policewoman and former paramedic. Using her life experiences and training, she strives to find the perfect mix of suspense and romance for her readers to enjoy.

Awards:

Wannabe in Wyoming (co-authored by J.B. Havens) won the bronze medal in the 2021 Readers' Favorite Awards in the General Romance category.

Scattered Moments in Time, won the gold medal in the 2020 Readers' Favorite Awards in the Fiction Anthology category.

The Road to Solace (formerly *The Friar*), won the silver medal in the 2017 Readers' Favorite Awards in the Contemporary Romance category.

Samantha has over thirty-five books published throughout several different series as well as a few standalone novels. A full list can be found on her website.

Sexy Six-Pack's Sirens Group on Facebook
Website: www.samanthacoleauthor.com
Newsletter: www.samanthacoleauthor.-
com/newsletter-signup

facebook.com/SamanthaColeAuthor
instagram.com/samanthacoleauthor
bookbub.com/profile/samantha-a-cole
goodreads.com/SamanthaCole
amazon.com/Samantha-A-Cole/e/B00X53K3X8

www.ingramcontent.com/pod-product-compliance
Lightning Source LLC
Chambersburg PA
CBHW030000010826
48973CB00007B/2101